OCEAN LANDING

OCEAN LANDING

DANGEROUS GAMES

**A Serialized Novel by
Wesley Adams and Daphne McGee**

Book 7 of the Soap Opera Inspired Story Collection
Series Created by Gary Brin

Episodes 1-7

Standish Press

The serialized story in this novel is fiction. Real persons, geographical locations, books, television shows, films, music, and specific events mentioned or which appears as part of the multi-character ensemble in this story were dramatized for entertainment purposes only and have no actual connection to fictional characters and created storylines in this book or reflects upon actual reality of things that may have happened previously or of which seems somewhat similar to real-life situations.

Names of real people mentioned in this book are in bold letters.

Select comments by fictional characters in this novel about historical figures, true crime cases, and, or pop culture icons are based on fact and additional information can be found online in reputable sites as well as numerous published books.

Several characters from the novels *Glass Owl*, *Desperate Lives*, *Thomas Nix*, *Ocean Landing* and *Games People Play* appear in this story as part of the storyline. All of the novels mentioned above are original publications from Standish Press and part of the Soap Opera Inspired Story Collection Series.

Not everything is what it seems—but some things are more removed from reality than imagined.

If something seems too good to be true it's because it's exactly what it appears to be—unrealistic.

Contents

Intro

Ocean Landing Dangerous Games continues the story of life in a small coastal town in California as local townspeople struggle with multiple dramas occurring at the same time resulting in complications that extend far beyond their picturesque seaside village. As with the earlier books in the Soap Opera Inspired Story Collection—existing characters and their stories from previous novels are intertwined in the present storyline of life in a small seaside village with plenty drama.

This is a soap opera inspired episodic novel written specifically to continue similarly formatted themes from beloved daytime soap operas as well as memorable prime-time soap classics—but with mature adult storylines added. Nevertheless Ocean Landing Dangerous Games was written to resemble a filmed YouTube web series and though it occasionally imitates traditional classic soap operas to a certain extent—it was written with the intention that it's playing to a visual audience and therefore will emulate a scripted format (without camera angle directions) rather than the usual storytelling methods displayed in popular full-length novels such as Malibu by William Murray and Master of the Game by Sidney Sheldon. It should also be noted that each episode of this series were written in a brief span of 6-12 days or less and therefore shouldn't be confused with being great literature. The goal of this series was simply to mimic episodes of modern-day prime time soap operas or filmed YouTube web series dramas—by creating visual entertainment on a printed page—and not to create a literary masterpiece.

The present storyline in *Ocean Landing Dangerous Games* takes place approximately at the same time the hunt for a mysterious key in *Games People Play* concluded. A few characters from the Soap Opera Inspired Story Collection Series are included in this novel as well to continue multiple unfinished storylines.

Gary Brin
Series Creator

In an effort to have an accurate portrayal of the dialogue used for the *Soap Opera Inspired Story Collection Series* people were anonymously observed in shopping malls, schools, places of employment, and on public streets in order to capture a definitive portrayal of how people of various ages and cultures interacted and talked to each other when they thought no one was listening. While some select dialogue was exaggerated for dramatic purposes when needed—the manner and tone of which people were observed speaking to each other in casual and private conversations is accurate. Exact wording was not copied verbatim for the most part, but the way certain types of topics and conversations are addressed by characters in this serialized series is based on actual situations that were observed over a period of several dozen years.

Prologue

Six Months Previous

A woman looks at a large collection of jewelry lying in a plain brown box. She seems upset as she stares blankly at the box unwilling to touch the sparking diamonds. Her boyfriend comes toward her and with one swipe he whacks her across the face.

"What are you waiting for?"

He raises his hand again.

"I want you to shop these for me."

The woman looks at him and seems uneasy.

"This isn't right. There has to be another way for us to get money from your dying aunt. She doesn't deserve to be robbed in her final days—how about we wait until she passes away."

The man seems about to explode.

"I'm tired of you trying to tell me what to do."

He sighs loudly.

"I have no intention of waiting until my aunt kicks the bucket. She could linger for months. I need money now."

The woman stands up and faces the man.

"I'm not stealing anything from that sweet old lady."

The man grabs her in a rage.

"I'll kill you—I swear I will."

He hits her hard across the face again.

"I've killed before—twice—one more time won't faze me in the least—I'm not the type of guy you want to insult."

He shoves her to the floor.

"Either you do what I say or I'll personally make sure you end up in a ditch somewhere with so many bruises to your face no one will ever figure out your identity without dental records."

He flexes his muscular arms.

"What's it going to be?"

The woman turns around and attempts to run to the door in a panic. But the man catches her and they struggle as he tries to wrap his arms around her neck. As they struggle she notices a metal vase on the table nearby and reaches for it. As he attempts to hit her again she whacks him with the vase. He falls backwards and whimpers briefly before he becomes still. The woman looks at the man lying before her for a few minutes and begins calling out his name. But there is no reply. She reaches over to touch his wrist and realizes he's dead. She screams and looks around the room. Tears stream down her face as she begins to cry.

2

"What will it be lady?"

The woman looks at the taxi driver and shrugs.

"San Francisco."

The taxi driver rolls his eyes.

"That's quite a ways away. It won't be cheap."

The woman sighs loudly and nods.

"I know."

The taxi driver looks at her and shakes his head. He looks at her again and seems confused by her erratic behavior. He gets into the cab and glances at her for a few seconds. He shrugs.

"I'll need half the money up front."

She looks at her purse.

"How much is it?"

The taxi driver looks at the woman oddly and silently begins checking rates on his computer and then tells her what he expects. She nods and hands him several hundred dollar bills. He slowly looks at her again and seems nervous. He sighs loudly.

"Are you in some sort of trouble young lady?"

The woman shakes her head.

"Of course not—I just want a fresh start."

The man smiles slyly.

"Boyfriend messed up didn't he?"

The woman nods and looks out the window.

3

Postcard perfect scenes of the Pacific coast whip by as a taxi drives past jagged rocks and bridges crossing scary-looking gorges. The woman in the backseat stares blankly out the window seeming to be looking at the scenery and enjoying the beauty before her but in reality she sees nothing as her mind continues to focus on the events that happened just a few hours before where her former boyfriend ended up dead. She finally snaps out of her self-induced nightmare as she sees words printed in block lettering on a sign at the side of a highway.

OCEAN LANDING
One Mile Ahead

"Wait. *Stop*. Take me to Ocean Landing instead."

The taxi driver turns to look at the woman and seems annoyed at her sudden change of plans. He pulls to a stop.

A Brief Look at the First Episode

Events from the past create unexpected conflicts for several residents while the realities of small town life dims the joy of living where everyone knows your name—as grim details from a recent tragedy come to light with few acceptable answers.

Return Engagement

1
Present Day

"You actually lived here as a child?"

Wiley Wilkerson glances at his wife and grins.

"Yep—my folks made their living hopping from town to town all over the Pacific coast teaching stage acting to denizens of small villages like Ocean Landing. I was actually born in Santa Barbara but have no memory of it. Nice place to live though."

Yvette Wilkerson reaches out to stroke her husband's cheek. At that moment there is a groan from the backseat.

"Oh God—not again—enough touching already. Go get a room already—no one should have to see old people touch."

Wiley and Yvette turn to look at their teenage son. He rolls his eyes and yawns. Emerson Wilkerson seems annoyed.

"Do you know how embarrassing it is for a guy to see his parents touching each other like a pair of teenagers—*yuk*."

Yvette grins broadly.

"If it wasn't for us touching each other you wouldn't be here today young man—deal already—learn to accept it."

Yvette reaches out touch Wiley's face again and then looks at Emerson. He rolls his eyes and seems disgusted.

"I think I may need a shrink."

Yvette laughs.

"Be careful what you wish for—I might take you up on your offer. Might do you some good to stop being so rude."

Emerson makes a gesture with his finger.

2

Rebecca Martin knocks on the back door of a house and waits. Several minutes later David Kipling opens the door and smiles as he sees his neighbor standing there. He instantly notices the wrapped casserole in her hands. He grins broadly.

"You don't have to keep feeding me Rebecca."

She smiles slyly.

"I want to. Since I closed my cafe last year I've missed sharing my cooking with everyone. I hope you're not upset?"

David waves his hand.

"I could never be upset with you Rebecca. If it wasn't for your concern I'd never have been able to deal with what happened to Melissa. You've helped more than you know."

Rebecca hands David the casserole.

"I hope you enjoy it."

He laughs.

"Oh, I'll enjoy it no doubt. I've put on weight because of your tasty cooking—not even **Julia Child** could best you."

Rebecca blushes.

"Oh, I could never be as good as her."

David looks at the casserole.

"I say differently."

He motions for her to come inside the house and heads to the kitchen. She follows David into the kitchen and waits.

"Losing Melissa was a shock but finding out about her dealings with Father William was quite a blow to my ego."

He runs his fingers through his hair.

"I just want you to know how much I appreciate having you next door—making delicious meals and listening to me when I needed really someone to talk to that wouldn't judge me."

Rebecca reaches out to pat David on the shoulder.

"I'm glad I could of help. You're like the son I never had. My late husband became sterile due to a painful war injury in Vietnam—and he refused to adopt after we married in 1975."

She seems about to cry.

"I've always wanted to have children of my own."

David reaches out to hug Rebecca.

"What would I do without you?"

They hug again.

3

Cyril Spalding leans back in his chair as he curiously looks at Jennifer Slater. She seems annoyed for some reason.

"What's going on with you? This is the third time in the last hour that you've reacted badly to hearing Susan's name."

Jennifer rolls her eyes.

"Susan Balfour is trouble with a capital T. That woman has a terrible reputation when it comes to seducing men. I just don't like the fact that she will be working so closely with you."

Cyril waves his hand in the air.

"I promised her already. I won't go back on my word."

He leans forward.

"You've got to trust someone at some point. Not everyone is out there lying and scheming behind your back."

Jennifer takes a sip from the mug of coffee in front of her.

"I'm trying—but it's hard after what happened."

Cyril sighs loudly.

"What happened with Peter Barkley is over. How could you know he was using you to support his addiction?"

He reaches out to touch her hand.

"I'm not perfect either—made plenty of mistakes."

He sighs loudly again.

"Ask any of my exes and they'll tell you how many times I screwed stuff up royally—but I'm trying to be a better man."

Jennifer pulls away.

"Let Susan know I'm watching her."

Cyril watches as Jennifer stands up. She walks toward the front door of the small diner without saying goodbye.

"A guy can only put up with so many mood swings."

As he turns around he sees Helene Jeffreys staring at him.

"I told you she had problems."

He shoots her a nasty look as she walks past him and heads to the door. Cyril slowly leans back in his chair again.

"Some people really need to get their own lives."

He shakes his head several times.

4

Karen Ewing carefully wipes the countertop clean and then turns to face her daughter. Carly Spellman shrugs.

"It's just been two hours."

Karen ignores her daughter and faces the front door again as she watches people walking back and forth on the sidewalk.

"Maybe this wasn't such a good idea?"

Carly walks over to her mother.

"What if no one stops by?"

Karen shrugs.

"Thanks for the vote of confidence."

Carly rolls her eyes.

"I'm a realist."

Karen looks at the front door once more.

"How about we hire a real cook?"

Karen faces Carly.

"I'd like to—if I could afford someone."

Carly seems lost in thought for a second and then smiles broadly as she seems to realize something. She grins.

"What about some sort of gimmick to boost sales?"

Carly pulls out her cell phone.

5

Jill Edmondson stares blankly at the computer screen as she watches several images fly by in front of her. She shrugs and seems frustrated. She taps on the desktop for a few minutes.

"Father William—who was he actually? Why did he pick Ocean Landing—did he pretend to be a priest elsewhere?"

She gestures with her hand.

"Maybe I should revisit his case and the murders."

She leans forward and begins typing.

"There are still plenty of questions left unanswered from what happened. Father William's death did not bring finality."

She pulls up a Google page and begins typing.

"It might be time to ask questions online."

She smiles as her fingers fly across the keyboard. Seconds later several stories about Father William appear. Jill leans forward as she continues searching for cached material about his murderous rampage. At first nothing appears—suddenly a large trove of files materializes on the computer screen. Multiple sites link older stories together with newer ones. Jill gasps as she reads several of the headlines from Los Angeles and San Diego.

"I guess it's time I chat with Colin Baxter."

She shuts the computer off.

6

"This can't be happening to me again?"

Daniel Williams seems upset as he nervously runs his fingers through his hair while he listens to the message on his cell phone from his girlfriend Cynthia Rodgers. He sighs loudly.

"Who breaks up on the phone?"

He shuts his cell phone off and leans against the doorway as he struggles to adjust to the bad news. He turns his attention to an orange tabby cat lying on the sofa. The cat gives him a curious glance as he approaches. He sits down on the sofa.

"Maybe it's time I spend time trying to figure out what I want to do with the rest of my life—before it's too late."

He looks at his cat.

"What do you think? What should I do?"

The cat gives an odd look and jumps down from the sofa and walks away. Daniel leans back on the sofa and sighs.

7

Jesse Malinger pulls away from Sabrina McCord after kissing her for several minutes. She gently slides her fingers across his lips and pulls him toward her. They kiss again.

"Who would've thought last year I'd be this happy?"

Jesse grins broadly.

"I could never have imagined."

Sabrina touches Jesse's face with her fingers.

"That's such a sweet thing to say."

Jesse pulls Sabrina toward him and kisses her.

"I've got a good life and a nice girlfriend."

He looks at the wooded area near the weather-scarred picnic table at the far end of Red Pine Regional State Park.

"When I first moved to Ocean Landing I really hated leaving all my friends and my life in San Diego. But you gave me a reason to like living in a small town—and it just took one kiss."

Sabrina reaches out to hug Jesse.

"I liked you from the moment I saw you."

Jesse notices several teenage boys entering the park.

"Here comes Lance Marler and his friends."

Sabrina turns to look and recoils.

8

Colin Baxter looks up from his desk and groans as Jill closes the door behind her. He wipes sweat from his brow and blinks a few times seeming to wish she was just a bad dream.

"How can I help you today?"

"I need info on Father William."

Colin seems disgusted as he sits back in his chair.

"I thought I made it clear previously that Dennis Bosley was not a priest and shouldn't be referred to as such. He was a cold-blooded killer and rapist. He came to Ocean Landing under false pretenses and then used the guise of a dead priest to kill over twenty-nine people over the course of two years."

He sighs loudly.

"As you recall he also killed his own his wife—whose bones we found on the outskirts of town. According to forensics she was badly beaten—bones broken in several places before he killed her using a block of concrete to crush her skull—then buried her body ten feet away from the highway leading out of town shortly thereafter. According to the secret diary he kept for years and of which we found hidden inside his house—he met the real Father William—William Thayer—about a mile down from where he had just killed his wife—and after the real Father William helped him fix a flat tire on his car he killed the kindly priest and assumed his identity when he arrived in Ocean Landing later that day."

She watches as he stands up.

"Can I see the diary?"

Colin looks at Jill and shakes his head.

"No."

Jill seems irritated.

"Is there a reason why not?"

Colin walks toward Jill.

"I don't have it."

Jill reacts.

"What happened to it? Did you throw it away?"

Colin looks at Jill curiously.

"It's at the FBI offices in Los Angeles."

Jill sighs loudly.

"Didn't you make a copy?"

Colin shakes his head and sighs.

"Of course not—why would you think I would?"

Jill glances at the empty office.

"I never said you did—I was only asking."

Colin walks to the door.

"The FBI closed the case after government sanctioned DNA tests confirmed the identity of Dennis Bosley and the fake Father William as the same person. His diary is at their offices in West Los Angeles. They took everything I had—all gone."

Jill seems upset and shrugs.

"Thanks anyway. I appreciate it."

She leaves. Colin closes the door behind her.

9

Larisa Lopez closes the back door of Pine Lodge Inn and walks out to the pavilion where her mother is sitting alone. Marta Lopez looks up and sees Larisa slowly coming toward her.

"I thought you said you'd take a break?"

Marta shakes her head.

"I lied."

She gestures with her hand.

"I'm almost done with the invitations anyway."

Larisa sits down next to her mother.

"How are you doing?"

Marta shrugs.

"I'm adjusting best I can."

Mother and daughter share a glance.

"I can't believe he actually sent you divorce papers."

Marta looks away.

"I'm over it—honestly I'm not in the least bit upset that your father wants to get married again to that cheap slut he left me for. They rightly deserve each other if you ask me."

Larisa stifles a laugh.

"I haven't spoken to him since he left town and moved to Seattle—and neither has Enrique from what he told me."

Marta shakes her finger at Larisa.

"He *is* still your father."

Larisa rolls her eyes and looks away.

"In name only as far as I'm concerned—that man brought shame to our family. A father—a real father would never willingly insult his family the way he did to us. He's dead to me."

Marta reaches out to touch Larisa's hand.

"How's Ward doing?"

Larisa smiles broadly and giggles.

"Wonderful—couldn't ask for a nicer boyfriend."

She gestures with her hand.

"He called earlier to say he was on his way back from a meeting in San Francisco. He seemed pleased that the condo deal went exactly as he wanted it to go—got a cool two million."

Marta raises an eye.

"He sold the condo on Nob Hill?"

Larisa nods.

"Uh-huh—he said it took too much money to properly maintain it year round. Sold it to a film director I think."

She glances at her watch.

"Oh-oh—I've got to go—got a meeting to attend."

Marta nods and watches Larisa walk toward the back door of the inn. She shakes her head and turns to look at the rose garden a few feet away. She smiles broadly and stands.

10

"Of course it matters that you slept with my brother a while back Nancy—why would you think I'd be fine with it."

Greg Williams digs his hands into the front pockets of his Levi's. He seems upset as he faces Nancy Baker. She sits down on the sofa without saying a word. He shuffles his feet.

"How long were you going to keep it from me?"

He slowly walks toward her.

"This *is* a small town—people talk."

He runs his fingers through his hair.

"What do you think would happen when I found out?"

Nancy turns to face Greg but remains silent.

"Do you think I wouldn't care?"

Nancy seems about to cry.

"It was only four times. We slept together four times and then decided we were better as friends. It wasn't anything that matters. There isn't anything going on between us now."

Greg walks back and forth.

"Is that supposed to make everything right?"

Nancy shakes her head.

"I'm sorry—how many times do you want me to say it."

Greg stops and faces Nancy.

"Sorry that you got caught or sorry you did it? There's a big difference in case it didn't occur to you beforehand."

He runs his fingers through his hair again.

"I need some air."

He walks to the door and stops.

"I don't know which is worse. The fact you slept with my brother or the fact you weren't going to tell me about it."

He leaves. Nancy looks at the door for a few seconds and begins to cry. As tears slowly fall from her eyes she notices several torn photographs lying on a table nearby and reacts.

11

Natalie MacDonald slides her hands across her boyfriend's chest and smiles as he notices. He reaches out to kiss her hand as they look at the waves crashing on the rocks a few feet away.

"Still think this was a lame idea?"

Natalie smirks and kisses Hardy Wheeler.

"Do you still think the two of us spending time together was a bad way to enjoy a day off from your crappy job?"

Hardy grins.

"I never said it was lame."

He brushes strands of hair away from Natalie's face.

"I clearly stated I was extremely busy."

Natalie glances at the ocean.

"Likely story if you ask me—you just wanted to spend the day sleeping. That's the real deal and you know it."

Hardy sighs loudly.

"I hate it that I can't pull the wool over your eyes and get my way—terrible for a guy who thrives on being sneaky."

Natalie kisses Hardy again.

"Do I hear you admitting to being sneaky?"

Hardy laughs.

"Got a problem with that?"

Natalie pretends to choke Hardy.

"What do you think?"

Hardy grins as he pulls Natalie toward him.

"I'm not sorry I lied."

"Do tell."

Natalie watches as Hardy stands.

"I think I'll go for a swim."

Natalie watches as Hardy runs toward a rocky cove several yards away. She quickly stands and runs after him.

12

"You were my girlfriend until *he* came along."

Lance Marler glares at Sabrina as Jesse seems ready for a fight with his rival. Lance faces his friends briefly as Sabrina makes a gesture with her hand and turns to look at Jesse.

"I've moved on—get over it already."

Lance turns to face Jesse.

"She's used goods buddy—sampled her wares plenty."

Sabrina seems disgusted by Lance's remark.

"You're a toad—a toad prince."

Lance laughs loudly.

"I'll take that as a deserved compliment."

He makes a lewd gesture with his finger.

"But better a toad than a slut who gives it away to any guy that pretends to care about her—I should've asked you how much the first time we fucked—might have made more sense."

Jesse takes a step forward.

"I think it's time for you to leave."

Lance laughs and clenches his fist.

"What if I don't?"

Jesse turns to look at Sabrina and then at Lance's friends who seem ready to fight. He faces Lance again and smirks.

13
Morro Bay

Jacob Allington leans back in his chair as Kyle Fairgate closes the folder in his hands and faces Jacob. He shrugs.

"It's the best I can do at the moment."

Jacob stares blankly at Kyle.

"What I gather from that very dull report is that I can't sue the State of California for what happened to my brother?"

Kyle nods several times.

"There are no loopholes in the law pertaining to Dennis Bosley and his murderous rampage which took your kid brother's life. He was just in the wrong place at the wrong time."

Jacob slams his fist down on the table.

"There's got to be a way."

He angrily shakes his fist at Kyle.

"I want my brother's death avenged. That freak killed my brother because California has lousy laws. I want action."

Kyle seems upset.

"What do you think I should do?"

Jacob sits up.

"That's what I pay you for—earn your fucking pay."

He walks over to where Kyle is standing.

"Or else I'll find someone else."

He walks to the door and motions for Kyle to leave. They look at each other briefly as Kyle walks to the door. He sighs.

"I can only do so much."

Jacob roughly shoves Kyle out the door.

"Tell it to someone who cares."

He slams the door to the office shut.

"It's nice to meet you."

Karen glances at Carly as Travis Penwick extends his hand.

"Karen Ewing."

They shake. He looks around the diner and shrugs.

"Not bad in general—but a little dull."

Karen looks at Carly again.

"Like I told you I have a limited budget."

Travis sighs loudly.

"It's not always about money. Making this place seem a little more inviting is free. Photographs on the walls are always helpful—even if those pictures are of you and your friends. Brings a warmer feel to a diner—live flowers is also a winner."

Carly slowly walks over to where Travis and her mother are standing. She turns to face the diner again and smiles.

"I think he's right."

Karen seems confused.

Maureen O'Bannon shrugs as she places the last box on the shelf. She turns to look at the overstuffed attic and sighs.

"One of these days I have to organize."

In the doorway Rebecca nods in agreement.

"I agree."

Maureen smirks as she faces Rebecca.

"Easy for you to say—your attic is spotless. The last time I was there is looked absolutely perfect—nothing out of place."

Rebecca rolls her eyes.

"What can I say—having lots of time on your hands make for a spotless attic year round—especially since I lost Langley to cancer. Quite therapeutic if you must know the truth."

Rebecca gives Maureen a knowing look.

"How are Gail and Andrew doing?"

Maureen shrugs.

"Andrew loves Boston and Gail is adjusting to life in Thousand Oaks. Said after what happened with Tyler she couldn't live here anymore—said the scandal was too much to face."

Rebecca nods.

"Did anything ever come from the investigation that Colin Baxter promised into Tyler's connection to the Russian mob?"

Maureen shakes her head.

"They came to a dead end with possible suspects. Tyler was in deep with every criminal type on the coast. As far as they're concerned this is just another cold case in the making."

Rebecca reacts to the revelation.

16

Los Angeles

"I told you I'm tired of this crap."

Laird Cooke slams the copy of a script down on the desk in front of him. Jeffrey Webber sits up and seems annoyed.

"You can't say no to Bastian Rego."

Laird shrugs.

"Watch me."

He walks to the door.

"I'm done with bad scripts. Tell Bastian he can shove this lousy script up his ass and then some. I'm out of here."

He grabs the doorknob.

"He'll ruin you Laird."

Laird sighs and faces Jeffrey. He makes a lewd gesture with his finger and grins. He watches Jeffrey's reaction.

"Ask me if I care."

He leaves. Jeffrey leans back in his chair.

"Sometimes I really hate being an agent—so many prima donna actors to deal with everyday—always complaining."

He looks at the scripts on his desk.

"That reminds me, I have to call Alden Washington. Got to keep him happy—especially with what happened before."

He picks up his cell phone.

17

"I'm not going to ask again."

Susan Balfour looks at Gary Barrington coldly as he stands in front of her completely naked. He grins broadly and winks.

"I don't like wearing a condom when I have sex."

"You'll wear a condom or else."

Gary looks down at his penis sticking out in front of him and makes a lewd gesture with his finger. Susan notices.

"What's the big deal—you're on the pill—aren't you."

Susan points to the door.

"*Get out.*"

Gary hesitates.

"I didn't bring any with me."

Susan glances at a ceramic box on top of a small table several feet from where Gary is standing. She smirks.

"I've got plenty—grab a few."

Susan watches as Gary reluctantly walks to the table.

"Pick one."

He begins combing through the tiny wrapped condoms inside the box. Susan walks over to him with a satisfied look on her face. She wraps her arms around his naked waist. He grins as he turns to face her. They kiss for a few seconds. He sighs.

"For the record I'm not a fan."

Susan rolls her eyes.

18

Carly closes the door and watches Travis walk down the sidewalk. Karen turns to look at the diner again and sighs.

"Maybe he's right."

Carly nods.

"He is—knows his deal—good reputation."

Karen notices Carly still looking out the window.

"Is he that guy you've been seeing on the sly?"

Carly turns to face her mother.

"I don't know what you're talking about."

Karen gives Carly a knowing look.

"Uh-huh—how long?"

Carly grins and turns away.

"Since Thursday—I met him at Safeway."

Karen sighs loudly.

"What about David Kipling?"

Carly shrugs.

"There was nothing there."

Karen walks over to her daughter.

"But I thought you said he asked you out?"

Carly seems uneasy.

"He did—but we never set a formal date when we'd get together for dinner. I think he's still hung up on Melissa."

Karen rolls her eyes.

"I still can't believe she was fooling around behind his back—and of all people—a demented serial killer to boot."

Carly makes a gesture with her hand.

"David is a nice guy—but way too trusting."

Karen nods.

"He would've been perfect for you."

Carly shakes her head.

"It's old news—OK."

They look at each other.

"Bring Travis by for dinner."

Carly smiles broadly and hugs her mother.

"He's a nice guy."

They look at each other again.

"He's from Ventura County originally."

She hugs her mother again.

"His family relocated to Monterey when he was ten."

Karen leans close to Carly and smirks.

"Just be careful—I don't want you to get hurt. Not everyone is who they appear to be—men can be charming."

Carly nods in agreement and sighs.

Gary lies back on the bed and sighs loudly. He glances over at Susan and grins broadly. He touches her hair.

"A guy could appreciate moments like this every day."

Susan sits up in bed.

"I'm not breaking up with Jared Wycroft."

Gary seems annoyed.

"Why not—you're just stringing him along—using him because he's got a ton of cash in the bank—but no game."

Susan rolls her eyes.

"He's a dud I admit—but a rich dud."

Gary pulls Susan toward him.

"I don't like being used."

Susan smirks.

"You have no choice in the matter—I call the shots—and don't you forget it—I'd pick Jared over you any day—easily."

Gary seems stung by the comment.

"Ouch."

He pulls away from Susan.

"You're cold—an ice cold bitch if you must know."

Susan climbs out of bed.

"I think you'd better leave right now."

Gary scratches his beard.

"I thought we'd go a second round?"

Susan points to the door.

"You thought wrong—one time is enough—I've got things to attend to—and people to meet—one of which is Jared."

Gary grabs his clothes.

"It would be a really sad shame if sweet Jared found out you and I was spending a lot of time between the sheets."

Susan reacts.

"Is that a threat?"

Gary makes a lewd gesture with his finger.

"I'm just pointing out a fact."

Susan watches as Gary pulls on his sneakers. Her anger is clearly evident as she walks over to him a few seconds later.

"Don't cross me Gary—you'll regret it."

Gary looks at Susan and stands up. He points his finger at her and seems enraged by her antics. He takes a step forward.

"That game works both ways in case you forgot."

He walks to the door and stops.

"I'm quite a popular guy with women in Ocean Landing."

He angrily slams the door and leaves.

20

Sabrina kisses Jesse for several seconds and then looks at him. She smiles broadly and kisses him again. He grins.

"I'll see you tonight."

Sabrina nods.

"Count on it. By the way, forget about the idle threats Lance made—he's just pissed he got dumped. His ego is bruised and he's just trying to deal with it at the moment best he can."

Jesse smirks.

"I'm not bothered—if he makes good on what he said he'd do—I'll be forced to teach him a lesson—San Diego style."

Sabrina nods in agreement.

21

Laura Stryker glances nervously at the envelope in her hand. She slowly twists it back and forth between her fingers.

"What could they want now?"

She slowly opens the envelope and gasps.

"This can't be real—what do I do now? I have nothing left after what happened. They took everything already."

She seems visibly upset.

"What should I do?"

She looks at the piece of paper again.

22
San Francisco

Ward Brady crosses a street in Nob Hill and is about to hail a taxi when he notices his ex-wife coming toward him. Claire Brady seems angry as she approaches Ward. He sighs loudly.

"Are you following me Claire?"

She shrugs.

"I'm been trying to reach you."

Ward seems annoyed.

"I thought I made it clear about where I stand."

Claire rolls her eyes.

"We need to talk this thing out."

Ward shakes his head.

"There's nothing for us to talk about."

He tries to hail a taxi.

"You cheated—not once—not twice—but throughout our sham of a marriage. I'm done playing games with you."

He notices a taxi coming toward them.

"My lawyer is handling everything. There's nothing for us to talk about anymore. We're done. Have a nice life Claire."

Claire watches as he gets into the taxi.

"I'm not done with you yet Ward."

She watches as the taxi pulls away from the curb.

"You'll be mine again—all mine. That I promise you dear husband—count on it. I'm going to get you back on my terms."

She clenches her fist angrily.

"But if I can't have you—no one will—especially *her*."

Claire slowly opens her purse and pulls out a cell phone.

"That whore can't have what belongs to me."

She begins dialing.

"That bitch is going to regret chasing after you."

She sighs.

"But first things first—revenge play."

She smiles broadly.

Laird nervously glances at his sister Cheryl Cooke as they drive along the coast heading north. She looks at the map in her hand and shrugs—then glances at her brother and smirks.

"I hope you know where we're going."

Laird rolls his eyes.

"Of course I know. We're still quite a ways away from what Simon said. He described it being past Oxnard on the coast."

Cheryl laughs.

"Ocean Landing is nowhere near Oxnard."

Laird sighs loudly.

"My bad—next time I'll know better."

Cheryl jabs her brother.

"I hope it was worth it to tell Jeffrey off. He's probably royally pissed at you right now after the way you behaved."

Laird sighs loudly again.

"He had it coming. I'm tired of the stupid scripts he gets for me. He knows I want to be taken seriously. Like really, how many times can they remake *Halloween*? It's laughable."

He glances out the window.

"Besides, I need to switch things up. Simon said Ocean Landing is real laid back—said it would be a nice change."

Cheryl makes a gesture with her hand.

"Is this the same Simon that got you into trouble every weekend at UCLA—the one who slept with every girl on campus and then couldn't figure out why he flunked a semester?"

Laird begins laughing loudly.

"Yep—one in the same—bet he hasn't changed. He probably spends more time on his back than any guy I know."

Cheryl seems upset and looks at Laird.

"I see I'm going to have to keep an eye on you just like when we were kids—and that goes for your friend also."

Laird gestures with his hand.

"Don't worry about me—I'm good—don't have time for a relationship—too much drama with Bastian at the moment."

Cheryl gives Laird a knowing look.

"That remains to be seen—I've seen what happens when you have too much time on your hands—seen plenty."

"This time is different."

Laird looks out the window.

24

"Where's Natalie?"

April Estes glances at Hardy curiously as he leans against her car. He rolls his eyes and reaches out to touch her. His hands slip under her blouse seconds later. He grins broadly.

"She's at home—so what—whatever. How about we talk about what the two of us can do together for the next hour."

He smirks.

"I can think of a few things the backseat of your car could be used for—exactly the same thing we used it for last week."

April pushes Hardy away.

"What if Natalie found out about us?"

Hardy rolls his eyes.

"What if she does—she knows we're not serious."

"Did she tell you that?"

Hardy makes a lewd gesture with his finger.

"Of course I did."

He grabs April without warning and pulls her toward him as she pretends to be upset. They look at each other and kiss.

"A dude has needs—you of all people should know that especially after what happened with you and that priest."

April pulls away from Hardy.

"Don't mention that man again to me—he ruined my marriage. He lied to me about who he really was just to get me into his bed—I almost ended up being one of his victims."

Hardy runs his fingers through his hair.

"Maybe it was a good thing your husband left. Leaves plenty of room for me to show you what good sex is about."

He pulls April toward him again.

"You're not supposed to be married so young anyway. Life has to be lived before you get tied down with marriage."

He kisses April.

"Take me for example—I got married in my freshman year in college and was divorced right after I graduated. It was a huge mistake from the beginning—like seriously, my bride actually expected me to be faithful. How could I be with just one woman when so many of my classmates were trying to get my attention each and every day I stepped out of our apartment? I was horny all the time. What did she think would happen? Of course I slipped up and began sleeping around. My wife didn't find out until she caught me screwing her younger sister in our bed."

He laughs slyly.

"I impregnated her sister by the way—which led to the two of them fighting over me and finally having her kick me out of our apartment—but whatever—best move I ever made."

He kisses April again.

"I saw her about a year ago in Las Vegas. She was still pissed at me. Said her sister kept the baby—said she wouldn't get an abortion despite the fact I wasn't in the picture anymore."

They look at each other.

"You've got a kid out there?"

Hardy nods.

"Uh-huh—must be a teenager now. Probably about fifteen or so—bet he's quite the looker because of who his father is—I'm quite a hot guy if I do say so myself—always been pleasant on the eyes—best thing about being me is my good looks—well, that and the fact I'm really a wonder in bed—chicks totally dig me."

April pushes Hardy away and sighs.

"You've got a gigantic ego don't you?"

Hardy laughs loudly.

"Got a problem with that?"

He reaches out to stroke her cheek.

"How about we get together like I suggested? I could show you a really good time—explore all sorts of positions."

April looks back at the supermarket.

"I like Natalie. I feel bad about stepping out with you behind her back. She's been through a lot in the last year. Losing her brother was a terrible shock. His death really put her in a bad way for months—she doesn't deserve anymore bad news."

Hardy waves his hand in the air.

"Warren MacDonald got what he deserved. All he did was blackmail people his entire life. Sooner or later that kind of crap catches up with you—and apparently for him it did. From what I heard he got snuffed out royally somewhere in Utah. He was blackmailing this rich bitch who was fooling around behind her husband's back with a whole bunch of dudes and one of them apparently took Warren out when he found out what kind of sick game he was playing. When I heard about it I wasn't shocked—I expected it sooner if you must know the truth—he was playing a dangerous game and it caught up with him—end of story."

April reacts.

"How can you be so cruel?"

Hardy seems shocked at the comment.

"Cruel? I'm not cruel April. I'm just stating facts."

He leans against the car again.

25
San Francisco

"That's right. He did it. He beat me up several times during the time we were married. He's a lunatic—a nutjob."

Claire sits back on the sofa and smirks.

"I know what I'm up against."

She sighs loudly.

"I want more money."

She gestures with her hand.

"Don't talk to me about this sounding like a plot right out of that old TV series *Pasadena*. I want him to pay dearly."

She looks at the large clock on the wall.

"If I have to find another lawyer to help me I will."

She stands up and walks to the window.

"I'm going to make Ward pay—and I'll start with that trashy whore he's been shacking up in a dinky town called Ocean Landing. I was told it's somewhere on the coast north of Los Angeles from what my friend said—near Morro Bay I think."

She rolls her eyes.

"I'll be expecting a call tomorrow."

She looks at her cell phone.

"I want Ward to know I mean business."

She laughs.

"I'll crucify him if need be."

She pauses for a few seconds.

"Call me at eight."

She nods a few times and hangs up.

26

Todd Zimmer looks at the baby in the stroller and smiles broadly as he looks up. Dorothea Wong seems pleased as she faces Todd. She watches as he begins playing with her infant daughter as a few onlookers walk by. They stop and notice the scene briefly and then keep walking. Todd looks at Dorothea.

"I still can't believe it."

Dorothea nods.

"Neither can I—Sean and I made a baby together and created a whole new life. It seems unreal—like a fairy tale."

Todd's face clouds over suddenly.

"How did Sean's parents take the news?"

Todd looks at the baby again.

"I bet they were not pleased at first."

Dorothea shrugs.

"They were better than my mother. She blew her top when she found out. But things happen. She's adjusted."

Todd seems upset at the comment.

"Things are just starting to calm down with me and Serena. Her folks are still in shock over Hailey's death though. It still seems like a bad dream—it's been really, really rough."

He looks at the stroller again.

"I was scared—what teenage dude my age wouldn't be when told he's going to be a father. It was a massive shock. I didn't know what to do—I felt trapped with no escape."

Dorothea pushes several strands of hair away from her face and sighs loudly as she faces Todd again. He looks away.

"It only seems hard at first."

Todd nods.

"Thanks."

Dorothea looks at the stroller again.

"Sean's parents want us to get married. Sean isn't so keen on the idea. Things it's silly to bother with a piece of paper."

"Serena thinks differently on that issue."

Todd wipes sweat from his brow.

27

"We're here."

Laird turns to face Cheryl as they see a small village bordering the Pacific up ahead. Several houses come into view as they drive toward the town. Laird grins broadly and sighs.

"It looks exactly like Simon described."

Cheryl sees less thrilled as she stares at the narrow streets up ahead. She turns to face her brother with a worried look.

TO BE CONTINUED

A Brief Look at the Second Episode

Several failed relationships from the past create problems for individuals in the present unwilling to move forward with their lives as other events begin to play out in unexpected ways when secrets reveal themselves at the worst possible moments.

One Day at a Time

1
Los Angeles

"I'm telling you my brother's death wasn't a result from some drug deal he was messing around with—he was murdered in cold blood—how many times do I have to explain this to you guys? He was knocked off by someone he knew—someone he trusted. Just do your work already and stop making excuses."

Edward Rolling wipes sweat from his brow.

"I want something done about my brother's death."

He shoots Leonard Masters a harsh look. The police investigator seems annoyed as he leans back in his chair.

"Like I told you several times already Rolling—there's nothing we could find to link anyone to your brother's death."

He sighs loudly as he notices Edward's stare.

"Face it—your brother was in over his head with criminal types and one of them bested him—left no clues behind."

Edward clenches his fists angrily and grimaces.

"In case you forgot I pay taxes to keep you employed."

He leans on the desk and glares at Leonard.

"I want you to get off your lazy ass and do what you're being paid to do. I'm tired of watching you guys only look for cop killers or people who snitched on one of your own. But rest assured no one is fooled. Everyone with even half a brain knows that the Los Angeles Police Department is the most corrupt police force in the United States—and trust me that says plenty when it comes to scummy behavior from police departments across this country. But let's look at the LAPD record in the last century shall we? In 1922 you guys let a murderer go free when **William Desmond Taylor** was murdered—and what about the 1935 murder of **Thelma Todd**? What about the rape case involving **Hal Roach** from 1937 when cops were paid off by studio executives? How about the 1947 **Black Dahlia** murder? I've heard endless stories about how you guys let evidence slip through your fingers. Of course there's that messy situation in 1959 involving the "curious" death of **George Reeves**. And then there's the notoriously suspicious 1962 death of **Marilyn Monroe** that we both know the LAPD were up to their eyeballs in covering up the truth in order to curry favor with **Robert Kennedy**. Oh, and what about what happened to **Bobby Fuller** in 1966—no one believes the official story you guys cooked up by the way—care to elaborate on what really happened the day his body was found and exactly how involved were the police in silencing the truth from coming out because of hush money they took to look the other way? And last but not least, why didn't the LAPD arrest **Robert Wagner** for murdering **Natalie Wood** in 1981? We all know he pushed her off their boat and let her drown. The fact he refused to discuss the case when asked was a clue that you guys *should* have acted upon. But still you dragged your feet and pretended it was all a tragic accident. My question is simple—how much did he pay the LAPD to pretend it wasn't murder?"

Leonard seems about to explode as he looks at Edward.

"How dare you talk to me like that?"

Edward smirks and leans closer to Leonard.

"Truth hurts doesn't it?"

He leans even closer.

"I'm tired of waiting for answers."

He looks directly at Leonard and sighs.

"If you don't find my brother's killer I'm going to make your life a living hell. Count on it. I want results within a week."

He stands up and looks at the door.

"In case you were thinking of finding weak points in my character—remember who you're dealing with before you act and make things worse. My brother may have lived life on the wrong side of the law—but I don't have such issues. I'm a state senator and you're a lowly police officer—and don't you forget it."

He walks to the door and stops.

"Your job is hanging by a thread Masters."

He smirks slyly and slowly makes a slashing gesture with his finger across his throat as he reaches for the doorknob.

2

"I can't believe you actually showed your face."

Simon Andrews reaches out to hug Laird Cooke as his sister glances at the small office. Simon turns his attention to Cheryl Cooke and hugs her warmly. They look at each other.

"It's been ages."

Cheryl nods.

"It has—ten years plus."

She sighs.

"You were quite the wild guy."

Simon shakes his head and faces the office.

"I've matured."

He winks at Laird knowingly.

"What about you? Who's been in your bed?"

Laird rolls his eyes.

"I'm been flying solo since my wife split."

He turns to look at the office again and shrugs.

"She wanted me to get serious about making a baby and I wasn't ready—I wasn't ready for the house and picket fence."

He sighs loudly and gestures with his hand.

"We're still friends—sometimes anyway."

Simon nods.

"Uh-huh—that's not what I heard."

He jabs Laird.

"I heard you skipped around with one of her friends."

Laird looks at Cheryl and then at Simon.

3

"I want him to pay."

Lance Marler pounds his fist on the dashboard of his car as he looks at Andy Archer. He shakes his fist in the air angrily.

"He insulted me—he has to be taught a lesson."

Andy rolls his eyes at his friend.

"Get over it already—like you said, she's used goods."

He laughs and wags his finger at Lance.

"You popped her cherry—treated her like a cheap whore."

He makes a lewd gesture with his finger.

"Why do you care if she's screwing Malinger?"

Lance glares at Andy.

"I don't want her to have someone in her life—I want to be able to call on her and have my dick serviced on my terms."

He clenches his fist again.

"That rutty punk is sniffing around my property."

He slams his fist against the dashboard again.

"I want to hurt him badly for insulting me the way he's done by going after my girl—he's a marked man—DOA."

Andy looks at Lance oddly.

"I think you'd better chill out Lance. If anyone heard you talking like that they might get the wrong idea about you."

Lance faces Andy. His rage is clearly evident.

"I'm going to kill Malinger."

He suddenly grabs Andy by the collar.

"I'm going to kill that bastard."

Andy pushes Lance away.

"You better cool your jets before it's too late."

He sighs loudly and seems nervous.

"Your acting crazy about this situation with Malinger and Sabrina McCord—get a grip already—come back to reality."

Lance shakes his head.

"He's got to die."

He looks at Andy with an odd look.

"I want him in a box lying under a pile of dirt."

He smirks and shakes his fist.

"It would be so easy to take him out."

He shakes his fist again.

"No one would suspect foul play when he turns up dead on the beach—drowning would be assumed and then it's over."

He grins broadly and faces Andy again.

"I'll expect your help in taking Malinger out."

Andy reacts in shock.

4

Carly Spellman watches as Travis Penwick talks to Jill Edmondson on the narrow cobblestone street leading toward a small shopping center. Jill glances at Carly several times as she and Travis talk. She notices the chilly behavior from Carly.

"I can't believe you came back to Ocean Landing after all these years Travis —I thought I'd never see you again."

"I had my fill of Seattle. It rains too much."

They look at each other.

"I'm really glad you came back."

Travis nods.

"I'm glad to be back."

Carly watches as Jill and Travis hug.

"I'll catch you later."

"See that you do."

Travis nods and watches Jill walk away.

"She hasn't changed one bit."

Carly seems upset. Travis turns to face Carly and sighs loudly as he notices her harsh glare. He smiles broadly.

"What's wrong?"
Carly makes a barfing gesture.
"She's full of herself—snooty to the max."
Travis laughs nervously.
"Jill Edmondson is not a snob."
Carly shrugs.
"She is—a bit bitchy too."
Travis turns to look at Jill as she walks down the sidewalk and begins talking to several people. He faces Carly again.

5

Larisa Lopez hugs Ward Brady warmly as he enters the house. They look at each other briefly. She seems pleased.
"I'm glad you're back."
Ward looks at Larisa curiously.
"You don't like being in the house alone?"
Larisa shakes her head.
"It's eerie walking around hearing my footsteps."
Ward grins broadly.
"What about the ghost?"
Larisa rolls her eyes at Ward.
"There's no ghost."
Ward looks at the staircase and grins.
"Are you sure about that?"
Larisa gently shoves Ward as he begins laughing.
"I grew up in an old house not far from here in case you forgot—lots of weird sounds to be heard at night—but no ghosts to be found—and believe me as a kid I looked—and hoped."
Ward takes a step forward.
"That's not what I heard."
He notices Larisa's reaction to his comment.
"The real estate agent told me stuff."
Larisa grabs Ward by the arm.
"I was there remember—nothing of the sort happened."
Ward begins laughing.

Page 46 of 190

"Well, it could be true?"

Larisa pulls Ward toward her.

"Not one more word about ghosts."

Ward kisses Larisa.

"I can't promise any such deal."

He kisses Larisa again.

"I've got lots of ideas on the subject."

Larisa traces her fingers over Ward's lips and smirks.

"The only ideas I want you to be thinking about is what you're planning to do to me tonight in our bedroom."

Ward looks at Larisa and feigns shock.

"I might need some lessons."

Larisa kisses him again.

"Is that so?"

Ward nods several times and laughs.

6

"This place sucks."

Wiley Wilkerson turns to look at his teenage son.

"I'm going to ignore that comment."

Wiley turns to face his wife. Yvette Wilkerson shoots her son a look and faces Wiley again. They look at the thick coating of dust on the kitchen table of their new house. The kitchen gives the impression it hasn't been used in years. Emerson Wilkerson stops briefly as he looks out the window and notices huge waves crashing against a pile of jagged boulders about fifty feet from the house. He seems intrigued and steps closer to the window for a better view. Wiley and Yvette notices Emerson's reaction.

"I guess this won't be so bad after all."

He turns to face his parents.

"But I'm still not cool with you two touching each other like a bunch of teenagers. People talk—ugh—like just deal."

Yvette walks over to where Emerson is standing.

"Would you rather us fight?"

Emerson rolls his eyes.

"Like don't play reverse psychology on me—I'm on to your game—I just don't want either of you to embarrass me when we're out in public. It's going to be hard enough to adjust—but your behavior will cause me to become a target of ridicule."

"OK—OK—we'll curtail our behavior in public."

Yvette glances slyly at Wiley.

"We'll try."

Emerson sighs loudly.

The Next Day

7

Claire Brady rolls her eyes as she looks at the narrow hallway of the boutique hotel. She turns around and sighs loudly as she slides a plastic card into a thin slot on the door of her hotel room. As the door opens she gasps in shock at the tiny room.

"Damn Ward for not giving me enough money."

She walks toward the drapes at the other end of the room and pulls them open. She sighs loudly and turns around.

"I will get him back."

She grimaces.

"I'll have my way no matter what I have to do."

She smirks.

"But first things first—I've got to get that bitch away from him. She needs to know her place—stealing another woman's man is not allowed. She'll pay for her sins—and pay dearly."

She clenches her fists several times.

"The only question left to answer is how to teach that trashy whore a lesson she won't forget. It has to be something terribly cruel—highly unpleasant—maybe even dangerous."

She looks out at the small village in front of her.

"Uh-huh—this nobody town will certainly come to know my name soon enough—and so will Ward's new girlfriend."

She turns away and glances at the kitchenette as a stack of knives catch her attention. She walks over slowly.

"Oh yes—these will do nicely."

She picks up one of the knives from the wooden knife holder and looks at it as a huge smile creases across her face.

"Larisa Lopez had better watch her step."

She grins slyly.

"It would be such a shame if she accidentally ran into one of these—run into them and then couldn't call for help. Oh, such things can happen no doubt—horrible things happen every day when someone least expects it. I wonder if she's insured."

She begins to laugh hysterically.

8

"I need to talk to you about Celine."

Cyril Spalding turns around and looks at Paul Yarmouth as he's about to open the door to his gym. He seems confused.

"I already told you—Celine and I were over and done once you slipped a ring on her finger two years ago in Santa Barbara. I said I wouldn't be disrespectful to you and I haven't. I'm a man of my word Paul. I assumed after all this time you knew that."

Paul seems irritated as he stares at Cyril.

"Don't worry—I take you at your word Cyril. You've been a good friend to me in the last two years. But that said—Celine has been seeing someone on the sly—again. After that situation with Tyler Hernandez I thought she was a changed woman. But lately I've been noticing her behavior is quite cagey when it comes to telling me the truth—and that can only mean one thing."

Cyril runs his fingers through his hair.

"I don't know how I can help?"

Paul notices a few people walking by. He sighs and waits until they're out of earshot and then turns to face Cyril again.

"I was thinking maybe you can talk to her and see if things can be worked out between us? I love her regardless."

Cyril seems uneasy and shrugs.

"Do you really think that's a good idea?"

He nervously glances at the front door of his gym.

"What if she thinks I'm interested in her? I don't want to go down that road—don't need the drama at the moment."

Paul looks at Cyril oddly and shrugs.

9

Gary Barrington grins broadly as photographs appear on his cell phone. He smirks as the compromising photographs of Susan lying naked in bed seem to tell a story. He laughs.

"Oops—I guess I forgot to tell dear Susan that I had these taken when we stayed in Napa Valley two weeks ago. I think it's time she knew how risky it is for her to threaten me the way she did yesterday—trying to shut me up is not a good idea."

He looks at his watch.

"Uh-huh—I think these will get plenty of views on the Internet. Poor Jared—he won't be happy when the truth comes out and he realizes he's been involved with a cheap whore."

He clicks send on his cell phone.

10

Hardy Wheeler shrugs as he opens the door to a small corner diner. He walks toward Carter Benning and extends his hand. They shake. Carter then motions for Hardy to sit down.

"I'm glad you could meet me on such short notice."

Hardy seems confused and sighs.

"I can only spare ten minutes."

Carter nods in agreement and pulls out his cell phone.

"I've got a task for you—one that you'll like."

Hardy rolls his eyes in dismay.

"Oh-oh—here we go again with the ugly girl deal. I don't do dogs—I've got a rep to protect. I hang with babes only."

Carter jabs Hardy.

"This one isn't ugly."

He shows Hardy a photo on his cell phone. Hardy looks at the image and seems indifferent as he faces Carter again.

"My former business associate is coming to town in two weeks—his daughter just split from her husband. I—I thought you could keep her company while she's in town for a week—make her feel welcome as only you can—I'm willing to pay plenty."

Hardy looks at Carter curiously.

"This cousin thing is really getting old Carter—just because we're related doesn't mean you can pimp me out."

Carter smirks and puts his cell phone away.

"I never thought of you as an escort despite how you phrased my question. I never asked for you to sleep with her."

He grins broadly.

"She's a good girl—not like your usual girlfriends."

He makes a lewd gesture with his finger.

"Especially the ones you pick up at that sleazy bar out on the highway—Alicia Melendez is sweet and intelligent."

Hardy rolls her eyes again.

"Was that even her in the picture you just showed me? The girl you just described doesn't resemble that picture."

Carter seems upset and sighs loudly.

"Why would I lie to you?"

Hardy gives Carter a curious look.

"This Alicia person better not be someone dogs will howl at in public. I swear I'll seriously hurt you if you're lying to me."

Carter grabs Hardy by the arm.

"I'll double what I was intending to pay you."

Hardy looks at Carter and sighs. He makes a gesture with his hand and lowers his voice as he leans closer to Carter.

"This is low—like really low."

Carter seems desperate. Hardy notices.

"Triple."

Carter seems upset as he looks at Hardy. After a few seconds he shakes his head in agreement. Hardy grins.

"You owe me one Carter. I won't forget it. Especially if I end up with dog patrol concerning this girl you said is pretty."

Carter nods several times.

11

Emerson closes the kitchen door behind him and turns to face the backyard leading to the beach several feet away.

"I wonder if there are any kids my age that lives in those houses I saw on the way—anyone other than old people."

He sighs as he begins walking along the beach toward several large boulders. As waves crash angrily against the rocks he sighs loudly. The beach is completely deserted except for a few birds looking for small fish caught in nearby tide pools.

12

Larisa awakens and looks at Ward lying next to her. He's sound asleep. She smiles and slowly climbs out of bed. She pulls on a robe and heads to the door. She stops and looks at Ward for a few seconds and then leaves. Larisa slowly walks down the stairs and heads into the kitchen as she hums softly. She pulls open the door to the refrigerator and is about to grab a jug of milk when Ward's cell phone begins to ring. Larisa walks over to where it is lying on the counter and is about to pick it up when the call stops. Several seconds later it begins to ring again and then sounds of someone breathing on the other end can be heard when the answering service picks up. Larisa looks at the cell phone curiously. She seems bothered and is about to pick up the phone when it stops. She looks at it for a few seconds and then shrugs. Larisa glances at the staircase briefly as she slowly leans against the sink. She looks at the cell phone and sighs loudly.

"Who can that be at this hour in the morning?"

She looks at the cell phone again and seems to be waiting for it to begin ringing again. She finally looks away as she hears a rustling sound and sees Ward standing at the top of the staircase looking at her. He seems puzzled as he comes toward Larisa.

"What's going on?"

Larisa shakes her head and glances at the cell phone still a bit confused. She notices a look of concern on his face.

Page **52** of **190**

"Your phone just rang—and there seemed to be someone on the other end—but they didn't speak. They called twice."

Ward shrugs and leans over to kiss Larisa.

"Someone probably misdialed."

Larisa nods.

"I guess."

She watches as he pulls the refrigerator door open.

"What are your plans for today?"

Ward turns around.

"I'm not sure yet."

He grins slyly.

"Maybe spend the day in bed."

He pulls Larisa toward him and laughs.

"Have you thought about what I asked you?"

Larisa rolls her eyes.

"My father is off limits."

Ward kisses Larisa.

"Is he?"

Larisa looks away.

13

"I thought you were over Malinger?"

Lance shakes his head and slowly pulls to a stop. He faces Andy and clenches his fists several times. He sighs loudly.

"No one will suspect he didn't drown."

He grins broadly.

"We'll hold him under the water until he kicks it. Watch him gasp for his last breath as I laugh watching him die."

They both step out of the car.

"I'm not killing anyone."

Lance grabs Andy by the throat.

"Oh yeah you will."

He tightens his grip around Andy's throat.

"You don't have a choice. That jerk has shamed me for the last time—he needs to pay—pay dearly—pay with his life."

He seems to enjoy watching the look on Andy's face as he tightens his grip further. He laughs as Andy gasps for air.

"You'll help me or else I'll spill the beans on what you did last year—I'm pretty sure cheating on an exam is grounds to get someone expelled from school—it would be such a shame if somehow that info became public knowledge. Think of what would happen to your family—the shame would destroy your mother—cause her to get fired from her job at the bank."

Andy pushes Lance away.

"You creep."

Lance laughs.

"That's right—I'm a creep all right. But at least I didn't cheat on an exam. That's low—really low—and I will spill."

Andy seems to be looking for someone as Lance grabs him by the neck again. He seems enraged and hits Andy several times. He grins as he coldly twists Andy's arm backwards.

"Who are you looking for?"

Andy grimaces with the pain.

"I told you I'm not killing anyone."

Lance seems upset.

"He's a fucking loser—a total zero. That dude needs to pay for what he did—pay for insulting me by stealing my girl without asking my permission and then flaunting it all over town."

Andy jerks free from Lance's grip.

"Malinger didn't steal Sabrina. You dumped her for Racine Gilbert a week after you took her virginity. If you recall she was really upset but you acted like she was yesterday's trash."

Lance rams his fist into Andy's face. Andy falls backwards as the blow almost causes him to nearly pass out. He seems in shock as Lance seems ready to hit him again. He wobbles.

"She didn't mind that I was screwing around with Racine behind her back. She knows I never promised I'd remain faithful to her while we were going out—but she knew she had to be true to me no matter what—she promised me she was mine and mine alone—until that frigging punk Malinger came to town."

He lashes out at Andy again.

"I'm not going to ask you twice Archer."

Andy takes a deep breath and suddenly bolts from the car. He stumbles halfway across the rocks as Lance jumps out of the car and chases him. As Andy scurries across the rocks Lance continues his barrage of insults and threats. Several times Andy stumbles but manages to avoid slipping as Lance pursues him until they get to the beach. Andy runs toward a lifeguard station several yards ahead. Lance stops suddenly. He seems upset.

14

Chase Doubleday looks at the computer in front of him as his fingers fly across the keyboard while Todd Zimmer hovers behind him. He turns around with a worried look on his face as he faces Todd. He shakes his head several times and shrugs.

"There's nothing—nothing new anyway."

Todd seems nervous as he sits down across from Chase.

"But you said you could find more info on that nutjob that killed Hailey—you said there were endless stories online."

Chase wipes sweat from his brow.

"Serena and her family need closure for Hailey."

Todd stands up.

"What do I do now?"

Chase shrugs.

"Father William—also known as Dennis Bosley—was a serial killer with a list of victims stretching from San Diego to Ocean Landing—probably spent time in San Francisco too—stuff will show up eventually—people will talk at some point."

Todd runs his fingers through his hair.

"I promised her."

Chase leans back in his chair.

"It's not your fault—there isn't anything other than what was out there already. This dude was under the radar for years from what it seems. Hailey was just one of his many victims."

Todd walks toward a window several feet away.

"I just wanted to be helpful."

He looks at the computer screen.

"Are there any books written yet on what happened?"

Chase looks at Todd oddly.

"Not that I can see—this case wasn't front page news by any means—too many other stories occurring at the time. CNN no longer focuses on every breaking story like they used to."

He watches Todd's reaction.

"I think the best you can do is wait—the Internet is a wonderland for information. Every day something new pops up on stuff many people forgot long ago. Just look at the cases of **Martha Moxley, Robert Piest, Jacob Wetterling, Glen Albert Pritchett, Nicholas Markowitz** and **Irene Garza** among others. Their murders took time to solve but were solved nevertheless when new evidence surfaced—decades later in some cases."

Todd shrugs.

"Maybe I should talk to the police?"

Chase shakes his head.

"FBI handled the case not the Ocean Landing PD."

Todd stands up as Chase watches him curiously unsure about what to do next just as Todd's cell phone rings.

15

"Of course I didn't tell Gary to upload those photographs to the Internet. *Oh God*—I swear I'm going to kill him."

Susan Balfour walks back and forth as her rage builds.

"I know you told me he was a creep."

She walks over to the computer and turns it on. Seconds later she looks at the screen. She begins cursing loudly as she sees several photographs of her and Gary in various sexual positions. She seems about to explode as she sits down.

"He'll regret tangling with me—I'll make him pay dearly."

She looks at her watch and then at her cell phone.

"Of course I know I'm royally fucked if Jared sees these photographs. He'll never understand—what man would?"

She sighs loudly as she clenches her fist.

"Uh-huh—I'm thinking about Rodney Royer. He and I are still tight—he'll teach Gary a lesson and then some—break a few bones just for good measure—Gary needs to learn when I make a threat I mean it—and Rodney's just the guy for the job."

Susan grins broadly and nods.

"Yes—today."

She shuts off the computer and stands up.

16

"This link was just sent to my email."

Jared Wycroft looks at the photographs on the computer screen. He seems in shock and turns to look at his assistant.

"Call Susan—we have to talk."

Bernard Grable nods and begins dialing.

17

Rebecca Martin stops in front of a small diner and shrugs before she slowly pulls open the door and stops. She pauses a few seconds and then casually walks inside. She sighs loudly.

"Rebecca?"

She turns to see Karen Ewing coming toward her from the storeroom. They look at each other. Rebecca shrugs.

"I thought it would be busy?"

Karen nods knowingly.

"You and me both—but alas business is dead—seems no one wants to come in here for a bite. I'm at a loss for a reason if you must know. Hired someone to help—he said the place gave off a dull feeling—no warmth whatsoever. I think he may be right—but I don't know what to do—money is really tight."

Rebecca looks at the tray in her hand.

"I brought these by straight from my oven."

Karen looks at the tray curiously.

"Is that what I think it is?"

Rebecca nods.

"It is—samples of some of my best work."

Karen smiles broadly and takes a peek at the covered tray.

"How would you like to save my diner?"

Rebecca seems confused.

"I'm not sure I understand what you're asking."

Karen gently grabs Rebecca by the arm.

"I'm no cook by any means. I think your cooking might lure people in here for lunch—offer them more than the usual burger and fries menu I offer currently—which at the moment has completely flatlined in the worst way if truth be known."

Rebecca looks around at the almost empty diner. One customer is sitting at a booth near the register. Rebecca grins.

"You actually think people will come by for me?"

Karen nods several times.

"People haven't forgotten your cafe on Elm Street."

They look at the customer sitting at the booth.

18

Rodney Royer grins broadly as he looks at the cell phone in his hand. He leans against the door of his car overlooking the bluffs perched high above the Pacific Ocean. He laughs.

"Of course I'll do it."

He looks at the brass knuckles in his hand.

"I'll gladly break a few bones in that loser's body."

He laughs again.

"No problem—you and I go way back."

He smirks as he looks out at the waves in a distance.

"When do you want me to hurt him?"

He begins laughing.

"No problem—Thursday is just fine with me."

He rolls his eyes.

"Of course I won't kill him."

He makes a gesture with his hand.

"I'll just make sure he's in serious pain when I leave his dump of an apartment after paying him a friendly visit."

He nods several more times and grins.

"A few broken bones would do the trick no doubt."

He begins laughing loudly.

19

Laird lays down on the bed in his hotel room as Cheryl looks out the huge window at the view. She seems nervous.

"What are you going to do about Bastian?"

Laird waves his hand in the air.

"He can go fuck himself for all I care."

Cheryl sits down at the edge of the bed.

"You've got to clean up this mess before Bastian starts spreading trash all over Hollywood about you. He can be quite spiteful when he wants to be. He's ruined careers before."

Laird sighs loudly.

"I don't care. His script is garbage."

He sits up.

"I'm tired of doing bad movies because Jeffrey wants to keep himself swimming in money. I need to take a stand before my career goes the way of **Marc Singer**. That guy had a lot of potential but let his agents pick stupid projects for him."

Cheryl seems confused.

"Wasn't he in the 1983 NBC miniseries *V* about aliens who try to take over the world—until they are unmasked?"

Laird nods.

"Uh-huh—he could've made it big in the movies but did one crappy film after another in the years following *V*."

He makes a slashing motion with his hand.

"I don't want to end up like him."

He stands and walks to the window.

"Besides I need a break from Hollywood anyway."

He looks at himself in a huge mirror near the window.

"I need to take stock in my life—in case you haven't noticed I'm not getting any younger. Give or take eight years I'll be forty. Forty is considered old by Hollywood standards."

Page **59** of **190**

Cheryl rolls her eyes and sighs knowingly.

"That only applies to women—you men have it made until you're in your fifties. Look at **Tom Selleck** if you don't believe me dear brother. Selleck became a household name when he was in his mid-thirties. Remained popular until he was in his fifties—and only became a has-been when he put on a ton of weight."

Laird laughs.

"OK—OK—I see your point. But things are different now for guys like me when it comes to continuous work—one or two bad movies can ruin you for years—kill your career instantly."

He wrings his hands nervously.

"I've got to make it clear to Jeffrey when I talk to him that I want good roles from now on—even if they're supporting."

He walks over to where Cheryl is sitting.

20

"Please Jared—let me explain."

Susan looks at Jared's face on her cell phone.

"It wasn't what it seemed."

She watches as Jared sighs loudly.

"Goodbye Susan."

The image on her cell phone goes blank.

"This is all Gary's fault."

She throws the cell phone on the sofa and walks to the kitchen. She looks at the sink filled with dirty dishes. Several sharp knives are sticking out among the unwashed items.

"That lousy bastard is going to pay."

She stops and begins smiling.

"Maybe Rodney will lose control and end up killing him."

She begins to dance joyfully around the kitchen.

21

Jennifer Slater and Cyril kiss as she turns to look around at the gym. Several trainers are working with clients. She shrugs.

"I came by to apologize about yesterday."
Cyril looks at her curiously.
"Is that so?"
He sighs loudly.
"This jealousy thing is getting old."
He wipes sweat from his brow.
"There's just so much I can put up with Jennifer."
He notices her reaction.
"The clock is ticking."
Jennifer looks at Cyril oddly.
"What's that supposed to mean?"
They look at each other.
"What do you think it means?"
Jennifer turns away.
"It sounds like I'm being dumped."
Cyril seems uneasy.
"It might be for the best."
Jennifer spins around to face Cyril.

"Is that your way of telling me you've already begun sleeping with Susan Balfour again? She's no good for you."

Cyril sighs loudly as he grabs Jennifer's arm.

"I'm not sleeping with Susan—she's busy with Jared from what I heard—and probably Gary Barrington also. I'm just tired of playing mind games with you over nothing—I'm miserable."

Jennifer pulls away from Cyril.

"I thought you were happy with me?"

Cyril shakes his head.

"I was—until you got possessive and began treating me like a piece of property. I put up with it as long as I could and then had to face reality—things aren't working—I'm really sorry."

Jennifer seems about to cry.

"I'm sorry. I didn't know I was such a horrible person to be around. I thought we were happy together. I assumed."

Cyril slowly walks over to where Jennifer is standing.

"You're not a bad person. I just think you need to figure out what you want before you try to be in a relationship."

Jennifer takes a few steps backwards.

"I'm so sorry I was horrible to you."

Jennifer runs out of the gym as Cyril watches her go.

22

Andy watches as Jesse Malinger walks into a small park across the street and stops to look at him for a few seconds. Jesse walks toward a bench shaded by several large trees and sits down. Andy looks at his bruised face in the rearview mirror of a parked car for a few seconds and then quickly makes his way along the sidewalk toward where Jesse is sitting. He looks up as Andy comes toward him. They look at each other for a few seconds. Andy sighs loudly and takes a few steps closer.

"You'd better watch out for Lance."

Jesse stands up.

"Did he send you to tell me that?"

Andy shakes his head.

"Lance is a freak. He doesn't take kindly to being bested by anyone. He has it in for you. Keep your eyes open."

Andy turns around several times as if someone might be following him. Jesse notices. He glances at the street nearby.

"I'm not afraid."

Andy nervously looks around again and sighs.

"You should be—he's dangerous."

He takes a step closer.

"It's up to you if you want to believe me."

He looks at Jesse again and then turns and walks away. He stops suddenly and faces Jesse again. He seems upset.

"Remember what I said."

He begins walking down the sidewalk as Jesse shakes his head not sure what to make of the odd encounter. He sighs.

"He's just pulling my leg."

He glances at Andy again and shrugs.

"Lance probably put him up to it despite what he said. But I won't be scared off—especially by a punk like Marler."

His cell phone begins to ring a second later. He looks at the name on the screen and smiles broadly. He sighs.

"What's happening with you?"

He watches as the screen opens.

23

Claire smiles broadly as she sees a Victorian house up ahead on a tree-shaded road. She grips the steering wheel of her rented car and turns to face the house as she drives by.

"This will be my home once I get rid of that damned whore. With her out of the way he'll come back to me."

She looks back at the house.

"No one gets between me and my husband."

Claire angrily slams her fist on the steering wheel.

"He and I belong together."

She pulls over by the side of the road.

"Everything was perfect between us until he met *her*. She is the reason Ward left me. I'm sure she bewitched him."

She turns to look back at the street.

24

Ben Allington shuts the door to his car and begins walking up the steep driveway of the Thomas home. He grins broadly.

"Today will be a first no doubt."

As he reaches the back door Astrid Thomas greets him with a look of confusion. He notices her reaction and sighs.

"Not the reaction I was expecting."

She takes a step forward.

"I wasn't expecting you today."

They kiss.

"Your dad didn't tell you?"

Astrid seems confused.

"Tell me what?"

Ben glances at the back door again.

"Your dad called me earlier and asked if I'd like to go rock climbing with him. I think his usual partner is sick with the flu and wanted to know if I could handle climbing a bunch of rocks."

Astrid rolls her eyes.

"My dad wants to hang with you?"

Ben nods.

"Uh-huh."

Astrid looks back at the house.

"Are you sure you want to hang with my dad for several hours? He'll probably drill you about what we do together."

Ben laughs.

"I have no intentions spilling my guts."

Astrid kisses Ben again.

"I'll hold you to that."

The back door slams and they turn to see Dexter Thomas walking toward them. Astrid gives Ben a cautious look.

25

Cynthia Rodgers looks at her watch again as she sits inside her car in a parking lot. She looks at her watch again and sighs.

"Where is he?"

Several seconds tick by.

"Where's Jacob?"

Cynthia turns around to see Kyle Garland staring at her with a curious look on his face. She gives him a harsh look.

"What do you want?"

Kyle leans against the window of her car.

"Who said I wanted anything."

He grins broadly.

"I saw you come into the lot and thought I'd just say hi."

He glances at his car parked a few yards away.

"I guess you finally found your Prince Charming in one of the Williams brothers. Lord knows you chased them both quite a bit in high school—of course you also chased me as well."

Cynthia shoots Kyle a harsh look.

"Is there a meaning to this pathetic trip down memory lane? Or is it that you finally realized what a toad you are."

Kyle pretends to be offended.

"Oops—you're in bitch mode today."

He laughs.

"I see you're still in a mood over what happened between us. Oh well, I think it would best serve you to move on and realize not every guy out there is stupid enough to fall for your lies."

Cynthia makes a lewd gesture with her finger.

"Get lost."

Kyle is about to reply when he sees Jacob Allington walking toward them from a nearby street. He looks at Cynthia again and gives her a knowing look. She ignores him.

"Uh-huh—I may be a toad—but Allington is certainly without a doubt the toad king. Wait until Daniel finds out you've been stepping out on him with the likes of Jacob Allington."

Kyle walks away but continues to look back every few seconds as Jacob finally reaches where Cynthia is sitting in her car. He shakes his head a couple of time as he watches them kiss for a few seconds. He seems disgusted as pulls out his cell phone and dials. He listens for a few seconds and grins broadly.

"It's me. We have to talk."

He nods a few times.

"I'll meet you in half an hour."

He gestures with his hand.

"I think there's something you need to know."

He looks at Cynthia and Jacob again.

TO BE CONTINUED

A Brief Look at the Third Episode

The seemingly perfect lives of those who live in Ocean landing begin to come apart at the seams when long-held secrets are exposed unexpectedly as the past and present begin to collide while two visitors comes to town with vengeance in mind.

Episode 3
Hidden Secrets

1

"Are you sure you're OK with this?"

Dexter Thomas turns to look at Ben Allington as he slips on hiking boots. Ben grins and stands up. He looks around.

"I'm OK with it all. Don't worry about me."

He watches as Dexter slips on his hiking boots. Dexter notices Ben looking at him. He stands and walks over to where Ben is standing. They look at a tree-covered hill in a distance.

"Climbing should take about an hour."

Ben nods and faces Dexter.

"I'm game."

Dexter reaches out to pat Ben on the shoulder.

"I just want you to know I appreciate you hanging with me today. Astrid isn't an outdoors sort of girl as you know all too well. Her mother was only into shopping malls—couldn't get either of them to go hiking with me no matter how much I tried to sway them on its merits. Having you come with me today is like having a son of my own—someone to do guy stuff with."

Ben smiles broadly.

"My dad never took me anywhere. He and I didn't really have a relationship. He was always somewhere up the coast."

Dexter looks at the hill again and sighs.

"For the record I'm sorry for being so rude to you when you first started dating my daughter. I was wrong about you."

Ben shrugs.

"It's OK. I know my family has a terrible rep."

He runs his fingers through his hair.

"I'm nothing like my father or my late uncle."

He looks at Dexter nervously.

"I'm my own person."

Dexter reaches out to pat Ben on the shoulder again.

"I know."

He sighs loudly.

"I couldn't ask for a nicer boyfriend for my daughter."

He jabs Ben and grins.

"Astrid is crazy about you."

A huge grin spreads across Ben's face.

"I sort of got that feeling."

Ben turns around to face the hill once again.

2

Larisa Lopez stares at her cell phone as it rings. She seems hesitant to pick it up. The ringing stops after a few seconds.

"Who's calling me with a blocked number?"

She glances at the back door nervously and then looks at the cell phone again. Less than a second later it begins ringing once more. Larisa sighs loudly reaches out to pick it up.

"Hello?"

There is no answer.

"Hello? Is anyone there? Who is this?"

The line goes dead seconds later. Larisa looks at her cell phone for a few seconds. She seems bothered by the call.

"This is the fourth time today."

She shakes her head.

"It's probably just some kid with nothing better to do."

She walks over to one of the windows in the kitchen and looks outside. Under one of the large trees in the yard she sees Ward Brady digging a hole. She smiles broadly and reaches for the doorknob. As she walks toward Ward he turns to face her and waves. Sweat drips off his body as she admires him clad only in cut off jeans. He walks over to her and points toward the hole.

"I think a few more trees are needed in this yard."

Larisa nods.

"I'm on board with this idea of the yard needing more trees if it means you're going to walk around without a shirt."

Ward grins slyly.

"I've gotten quite a workout."

Larisa tugs at his belt buckle and sighs.

"I've got wicked thoughts running through my mind."

Larisa begins to unbutton his jeans.

"How about we go back to the house?"

Ward pulls Larisa toward him and kisses her.

"I think you're asking for trouble."

Larisa kisses ward again.

"I'll take my chances."

Ward suddenly lifts Larisa into his arms and laughs. He begins walking toward the house as Larisa sighs loudly.

"There was another call earlier."

Ward stops.

"Someone called me again?"

Larisa shakes her head.

"I got a call on *my* phone—four actually so far."

He looks at her curiously.

"Did it seem like it was a crank?"

Larisa seems worried.

"I think whoever has been calling is doing it on purpose. I don't think it's random or a mistake. I think they know me."

Ward looks at the house.

"Could it possibly be one of your exes?"

Larisa shrugs.

"I don't think so. I'm on good terms with most every guy I dated since college—a few of them still live here in town."

They look at each other.

"But if it's not an ex-boyfriend—then who?"

Larisa shrugs again.

"Maybe someone who worked at the inn at some point is my guess. Nothing else makes sense to me at the moment."

Ward slowly carries Larisa up the stairs toward the back door and then puts her down as he reaches for the doorknob.

"I think we should call the police."

Larisa waves her hand.

"No—they'll ask too many questions. I think for right now we should just wait and see if the calls continue. If they do then I'll talk with Colin or Simon and see what they can do about it."

Ward shakes his head.

"I don't like it but I'll go along with whatever you want to do—nevertheless for the record I think it's a bad decision."

Larisa nods and leads Ward into the house.

3

"Old news—we're finished—she dumped me."

Daniel Williams looks at the beer in his hand and takes another swig as Kyle Garland sits down at the table. He sighs.

"Sorry dude—life sucks—but I guess you're better off alone than with a girlfriend like Cynthia Rodgers—especially now that it seems she's hooked up with Jacob Allington."

Daniel rolls his eyes.

"I've got the worst luck with women."

He sighs as he takes another swig of beer and notices Helene Jeffreys sitting alone at the other end of the bar.

"If I keep striking out I'll end up like Helene Jeffreys."

He begins to laugh.

"She's a real prize I bet. She's never had a boyfriend from what I heard. I think she's saving herself for the right guy—of course there will never be a right guy for someone so cold."

He snickers as he glances at her.

"Yep—I bet she's still a virgin. Still saving herself at her age—it's quite sad when you think about it—imagine never being popped and watching your life just slide by day after day."

Kyle runs his fingers through his hair.

"You're on a depressing ringer today no doubt."

He glances at Helene and then at Daniel.

"I think you've had enough."

Daniel looks at the bottle of beer in his hand.

"I've hardly begun."

Kyle takes the beer from Daniel's hand.

"Hey."

They look at each other for a few seconds and then Kyle forces Daniel to his feet. They walk toward the entrance of the bar as Daniel stops briefly to look back at Helene. He shrugs.

"I bet you anything she's a virgin."

Kyle shakes his head.

"What does it matter to you?"

Daniel seems confused.

"Do you think she would want to go out?"

Kyle turns to look at Helene.

4

Karen Ewing grins broadly as she looks at the line forming outside her diner. She seems pleased as she walks over to where Rebecca Martin is standing with her hands on her hips.

"I can't believe it—there's actually a line."

She looks at her cell phone.

"I think I might have to ask Carly to come by."

Rebecca looks back at the kitchen.

"Are they here for me?"

Karen turns to look at Rebecca.

"Of course—why else would they be here?"

Rebecca looks at the long line outside again and shrugs.

"Do you think that guy from earlier said anything?"

Karen makes a gesture with her hand.

"Uh-huh—he got one taste of your food and told everyone he knew in Ocean Landing. There's no other way to explain it."

Karen looks at the line outside again.

"I owe you."

Rebecca seems confused.

Two Days Later

4

"Are you sure this is the way to Ocean Landing?"

Julie Cartwright looks at David Sherwood nervously as they pass yet another sign. David looks at Julie and smirks.

"Relax already—we're not lost."

He laughs as he notices her reaction.

"My uncle will be pissed."

David laughs.

"You worry too much."

Julie shrugs and looks at waves smashing against rocks several yards away from the highway. She sighs loudly.

"I haven't seen him since his divorce."

She faces David.

"He told me he's in a new relationship."

David looks at Julie curiously.

"So?"

Julie rolls her eyes.

"I just want to make a good impression on her."

David laughs.

"Stop worrying so much."

He reaches out to stroke her cheek with his finger.

"Does your uncle know about me?"

"Of course he knows about you—knows we've been dating for the last two weeks. I tell my uncle everything."

David grins slyly.

"Does he know I was your first?"

Julie pretends to slap David.

"It's none of his business."

David turns to face Julie.

"You said you tell him everything?"

Julie pretends to slap David again.

"I tell him everything that happens to me at UCLA. I don't tell him about what my boyfriend and I do together. He's totally cool and wouldn't care less regardless. But I see no need to give him details of our sex life—especially with your rep being what it is around campus when it comes your list of conquests."

David makes a lewd gesture with his finger.

"What did you want me to say when we met—that I was a choir boy living a respectable life despite being surrounded by beautiful women—nope—I'm no saint—I've been around."

Julie reaches out and kisses David's hand.

"When I first told you I was a virgin—did it matter?"

David shakes his head.

"I wanted to be with you so badly that I didn't care one way or the other whether you were still a virgin or not."

He smirks.

"You teased me for quite a while when we began dating after we met at a party in Century City that one of my friends threw to announce his engagement to his girlfriend."

He grins broadly again.

"I tried to get you into the backseat of my car that night but you resisted—told me you didn't know me. I knew at that point I had to get to know you better. There was just something special about you that sparked my interest. We went out for a week before you let me spend the night at your apartment."

Julie reaches out to touch David's cheek again.

"You were so sweet—so charming. Wonderfully gentle with me knowing it was my first time. I fell hard for you that night if you must know. I knew from that moment onward I could never say no to you—and since then I've never regretted anything."

David looks at Julie curiously.

"I *do* care about you."

Julie reaches out to kiss David on the cheek and smiles.

"I've never doubted your feelings for me."

He pulls over to the side of the road seconds later.

5

Daniel curiously watches Jill Edmondson come toward him on the sidewalk. She seems nervous for some reason.

"Hello Daniel."

Daniel nods.

"How are you doing?"

Daniel shrugs.

"I'm OK."

They look at each other.

"How's the news business lately."

Jill shrugs and looks at her watch.

"I'm still trying to piece together what happened with Father William. He left behind more questions than answers."

Daniel nods again.

"He was a piece of work no doubt."

He sighs loudly.

"We had a killer living among us and we didn't know."

Jill nods in agreement.

"He committed a string of murders all over California from what I've been able to find. Didn't care if his victims were male or female—he killed simply because he seemed to get a kick out of watching someone die at his hands—he was a rapist too."

She waves her hand in the air and sighs.

"To think I actually talked to him and never knew he was a monster—makes me really sick whenever I think about it."

Daniel reaches out to hold Jill's hand.

"I'm glad you didn't know."

Daniel takes a deep breath.

"I wouldn't have wanted anything bad to happen to you."

Jill seems taken aback by Daniel's comment.

"Thank you—I appreciate it."

Daniel pulls his hand away and shrugs.

"I haven't forgotten."

Jill sighs loudly.

"I'm sorry about how it ended between us."

Daniel waves his hand in the air.

"I'm over it."

Jill reaches out to hug Daniel.

"I'm always going to have good feelings about the time we were together when we dated—you're a decent guy."

Daniel nods and notices people standing in a line down the street outside of a small diner. He faces Jill again and grins.

"I guess Karen finally got herself a good cook."

Jill turns to look at the long line of people standing on the sidewalk. She smiles broadly and faces Daniel again.

"Rebecca Martin."

Daniel turns to look again at the diner and sighs.

"I still miss her cafe on Elm Street."

Jill nods again.

"I second that."

At that moment her cell phone begins to flash.

"I've got to take this."

Daniel nods.

"I'll see you round."

Jill gives him a "thumbs up" signal and starts talking as he nods and begins walking down the street toward the diner.

"OK—what have you got?"

She seems irritated as she nods.

"I was expecting more info."

Jill shakes her head several times.

"I know—I know—these things take time to be found. I just wish it wasn't so tedious. You'd think with so many advances in technology that rap sheets would be easy to find online."

She glances at Daniel in a distance.

"OK—keep looking. I'm counting on you."

Jill seems annoyed and nods a few times and hangs up. She looks at the street for a few seconds and sighs loudly.

"I wonder if April Estes is ready to talk yet."
She looks at her cell phone.

6

Sabrina McCord smiles as she pushes Jesse Malinger down on a blanket and kisses him. He reacts and grins broadly.
"I guess you're happy to see me?"
Sabrina kisses Jesse again.
"I can't help myself."
Jesse laughs.
"Hey—I'm not going to complain if my girlfriend suddenly becomes aggressive and wants to have her way with me. I'm all for us guys not having to do anything in order to be kissed."
Sabrina kisses Jesse once more.
"I like you—like everything about you."
Jesse grins broadly.
"Tell me more—keep singing my praises."
Sabrina begins to stroke his hair.
"You're different."
Jesse sits up.
"I hope that was meant in a good way."
Sabrina pulls Jesse toward her.
"It was."
They look at each other.
"You're the first guy I've ever met that actually wants to know what I think—most of the guys I've known are dense."
Jesse seems confused.
"How else would I know if I didn't ask?"
He makes a lewd gesture with his finger and grins slyly.
"Do you know what I'm thinking about right now?"
Sabrina jabs him.
"We're not going to do anything like that in a park."
Jesse lies down on the blanket.
"I say we talk about it."
Sabrina playfully wags her finger at him.

7

"What's so funny?"

Astrid Thomas tries to grab Ben by the arm as he slowly begins walking down a rocky ledge overlooking the ocean where several stray cats come toward him from giant boulders nearby. He turns and grins broadly. He makes a gesture with his hand. Astrid seems frustrated as she watches him feed the cats one by one. As they rub against his legs he turns to face her again and mouths silent words she can't hear. She seems irritated.

"Why won't he give me a straight answer?"

A few minutes later he climbs up the hill to where Astrid is sitting and sits down next to her on a nearby rock. She quickly turns away from him. He notices and seems a bit bothered.

"Did my father say something mean to you?"

Ben stops and stands.

"Why would you think that?"

"Well?"

Ben grins broadly.

"We got along great."

Astrid stands up.

"Is that so?"

Ben nods.

"We talked about guy stuff."

Astrid turns around to look out at the ocean.

"You promised you'd never keep secrets from me."

Ben digs his hands into the front pockets of his Levi's and seems confused. He glances at the cats eating in a distance.

"I'm not keeping a secret from you. Honest."

Astrid wipes a tear from her eye.

"But you won't tell me what happened between you and my father when the two of you went hiking the other day?"

Ben gestures with his hand.

"Nothing happened. He was nice."

Astrid reacts.

"Did he ask about me?"

Ben shakes his head and grins.

"We talked about my messed up family—nothing about you. There's nothing to worry about. Like I said, he was nice."

Astrid pushes Ben.

"Are you telling me the truth Benjamin Allington?"

Ben runs his fingers through his hair.

"Your dad and I had a great time. He even apologized for how he treated me in the beginning when I first came by your house to meet him. Your dad told me I was the best thing that could've happened to you—told me I was like a son to him—made my day just so you know to have your father accept me for who I was and not who my father is. I thanked him several times."

Astrid seems pleased.

"My father said all that?"

Ben nods again.

"Uh-huh."

Astrid shakes her head.

"My father never apologizes for anything."

"I know—he told me he never admits to mistakes but felt he personally owed it to me—said he was watching me for a while now—and liked how I've made you so happy—said he knew losing your mother left a huge void in your life he couldn't fill—but was glad I seemed to have made you come out of your shell."

Astrid wipes a tear from her eye.

"Losing my mother was horrible. One day she was here and then she was gone. I was told she drowned at the gym on Grand Street but was never told why—or who found her."

Astrid runs her fingers through her hair.

"I found out afterwards she apparently had a stroke while she was swimming laps—and was found about an hour later when a swim instructor came in with several of his students."

Astrid begins to cry.

"It's been five years and I'm still not over her."

Ben hugs Astrid.

8

David holds Julie's hand as they lean against his car while cars zip by on the highway at breakneck speeds. He sighs.

"I know I have a rep."

He smirks.

"I've always had a rep—even before I came to UCLA after a few weeks at a college in San Francisco. Girls like me—and I like girls. I've slept with a lot of women—no use to pretend otherwise—I very promiscuous throughout high school when I lived in Castle Beach—I was known for being a backseat wonder wherever I went. I'd have sex with a girl and then be done with her right after we did the deed. I was wild—I admit it. But that was then and this is now. I've grown up a lot since I came to California—especially after what happened in New Orleans."

Julie turns to look at David.

"Exactly what happened to you and Parker?"

David sighs loudly.

"I'm not sure exactly—somehow we got mixed up with a bunch of crooks that were searching for a statue. It got really crazy for a moment or two for both of us—but the Feds somehow got wind of what was happening and busted a whole bunch of bad people connected with the Russian mob. A few of them escaped—went back to Russia or Europe from what I heard."

Julie seems confused at the statement.

"Some of those guys that tried to kill you are still out there somewhere—what if they came looking for you and Parker?"

David shrugs.

"I'm not worried. They were probably killed when they went back to Russia empty-handed. I heard one of them got busted for trying to desecrate a crypt of some politician."

Julie turns to look at the ocean.

"One of those guys who was after you and Parker got caught trying to break into a crypt to take someone's body?"

David nods in agreement and makes a gesture with his hand. He seems about to laugh but stifles it. He shrugs.

"That's what I heard. Plenty of stories out there about the grave robber's motives—local cable news outlets covered the incident endlessly. I think it was assumed the statue was in the crypt with the stiff—no one knows for sure—freak clammed up when they royally busted him—many unanswered questions."

Julie puts her arms around David.

"What about Castle Beach? Do you miss living there?"

David gestures with his hand and shrugs.

"Nope—don't miss it one bit—especially don't miss the winter storms that hit every year and royally fucks up everything. Of course there's also the "event" that happened in Castle Beach during my senior year in high school. It changed my life forever and changed Parker's life too—I'll never forget what I saw."

Julie looks at David curiously.

"You never told me about that?"

He shakes his head.

"Not much to tell—it was over before it began—but scary nevertheless—lots of weird things that can't be explained."

David shakes his head again seeming to try and shake the image from his mind. He looks at Julie briefly and then faces the ocean once more. He sighs loudly and faces her again.

"I still don't really know what happened actually—but somehow terrible nightmares seemed to come to life."

He slowly stands up and suddenly pulls Julie to her feet.

9

"Are you asking me out Cyril?"

Cyril Spalding nods several times as Sherilyn Matthews sits down opposite him at a corner booth while several people walk by and give them dirty looks. Several yards away they see Karen talking with a few of her customers. At the other end of the room Carly Spellman is also doing the same while several waiters brings out food as the lines seem endless on the sidewalk.

"What if I was asking you out?"

Sherilyn gives Cyril a curious look and smiles.

"I'm not the type of girl you like."
Cyril rolls his eyes.
"I'm just asking you out—no strings."
Sherilyn leans across the table.
"What about Jennifer?"
Cyril folds his hands in front of his chest.
"She and I have parted ways."
Sherilyn rolls her eyes.
"Good riddance."
Cyril seems upset.

"I know you didn't like her because she slept with two of your boyfriends—but that was then—and this is now."
Sherilyn seems annoyed.

"She did it because she wanted to spite me."
She sighs loudly. Cyril smiles as he sees Karen coming toward them with a huge grin on her face. Cyril shrugs.

"Hello Karen—I see you've got customers."
Karen nods happily.

"I should've hired Rebecca months ago. Can't keep people away—the place is in demand for the first time—popular."
She turns to look at the diner.

"Word got out that Rebecca was in the diner and suddenly lines started to form outside—made my day no doubt."
Cyril and Sherilyn nod several times.

"She's the best—I used to go by her cafe all the time when I was in high school. Her pastries were better than Sara Lee."
Karen seems pleased.

"I second that."
They continue talking for a few minutes.

10
Los Angeles

Leonard Masters looks at the files in front of him and seems worried as he flips through the pages. He sighs loudly and turns to look at Edward Rolling—and gives him the folder.

"There was no evidence found at the scene indicating the identity of any person or persons that might have been with your brother when he died. There were cameras in the building but they weren't working that day in particular. We are going to continue and look but we have nothing new at the moment."

Leonard leans back in his chair.

"I'm sorry."

Edward throws the folder down on the floor in a rage.

"I want my brother's killer apprehended."

He clenches his fist and shakes it.

"Dig deeper—I want results—or else."

He turns to leave and stops.

"I'll expect your resignation in two weeks if you fail me further—and don't bother looking to the police unions to help you. They've been warned already that any interference may result in me passing a law to disband their organization leaving the LAPD under the sole jurisdiction of the mayor—which would clear the way for useless police officers—from street cops to chiefs—being terminated for whatever reasons that are deemed just. Be aware I'll make good on my threat if you continue to drag your feet on this issue any further—consider yourself warned."

He turns and walks out of the room.

"Damn him—damn his loser brother to hell."

Leonard looks at his cell phone and sighs.

"He's put me in a really bad way."

He picks up the cell phone and begins dialing.

"I didn't want to have to do this—but Rolling has left me no choice but to act in a fashion that I wouldn't ordinarily."

He begins dialing.

"He won't let this go without help."

The line is picked up.

"Uh-huh—it's me—it's time we go to Plan B—seems Rolling thinks he's got the upper hand—or so he believes."

He gestures with his hands.

"I understand."

He nods several times and sighs.

Rodney Royer smiles broadly as he glances at Gary Barrington lying at his feet—his face bloodied from several recent punches to his face. Rodney lashes out again at Gary—kicking him in the chest several times. He laughs as Gary begs for him to stop. He jams his boot against Gary's face and smirks.

"If there are any more complaints from Susan I'll be back for round two—and this time I'll up the ante tenfold—I think we both understand what I'm saying concerning Susan."

He kicks Gary again in the face.

"Do we understand each other?"

Gary nods several times.

"By the way if you tell anyone about what just happened between us I'll be back—and my actions will just get worse."

He laughs and walks to the door.

"You brought this upon yourself—you deserve everything that I did to you—picking on Susan Balfour was a mistake."

He laughs again and leaves Gary's apartment.

"I'm going to kill him."

Gary looks at the door several times and slowly pulls himself up. He tries to stand and winces several times.

"Uh-huh—Royer is a dead man."

He cries out in pain several times as he stands up and looks around the living room of his apartment. Several pieces of furniture lie broken everywhere. Splotches of dried blood are scattered throughout the hardwood floor. He sighs loudly.

"That bitch is going to pay dearly."

He slowly walks over to the doorway and pulls the front door to his apartment shut. He winces again as he slowly walks to the kitchen. Gary grabs his cell phone and begins dialing.

"Let's see how she likes turnaround. That damn bitch has pushed me too far—and now she's gonna learn the hard way what happens when someone fucks me over—damn her."

He winces in pain again.

"Rodney had better watch out also—my friends won't play nice when they pay him a visit—not even a little bit."

He looks at his bloodied hands.

12

"Oh my God—it's really *you*."

Laird Cooke seems pleased as he looks at a woman standing in front of him. He raises his hand and nods.

"Yep—it's me."

Dorothea Wong glances at the stroller in front of her.

"I'm Dorothea Wong."

She sighs.

"This is my daughter Erica Wynne."

Laird nods.

"Have you lived here all your life?"

Dorothea nods.

"Uh-huh."

"I'm starting college next fall."

She looks at several people as they walk by.

"Are you here to film a movie?"

Laird laughs.

"I'm actually here on vacation."

Dorothea seems confused.

"You're vacationing in Ocean Landing? Why?"

Laird looks at Dorothea curiously.

"I just happened upon it."

Laird runs his fingers through his hair.

"It reminds me of a postcard."

He notices a few people nearby looking at him.

"How come you don't have an entourage with you like everyone else? It's just that everyone in Hollywood seems to have a whole bunch of friends hanging all over them all the time."

Laird looks at Dorothea oddly.

"Don't need fake friends hanging around me."

Dorothea nods in agreement and sighs.

"I loved your last movie."

Laird shrugs.

"It was OK—I wish I had more to do in it."

He sighs loudly.

"That's why I'm here—I need a break."

He looks around.

"Is there a place you can recommend that has really good food—not like those places **Gordon Ramsay** visits and instantly regrets once he sees how filthy the restaurants actually are."

Dorothea smirks.

"There's a place near my school."

She quickly pulls out her cell phone.

"I can give you the address."

Laird nods.

13

Gary walks back and forth as he talks on his cell phone. He stops and smiles. He leans against the counter and sighs.

"His name is Rodney Royer."

He shrugs.

"Uh-huh—that's exactly what I want."

He looks at the bruises on his arms.

"I don't care what you and your friends do to that jerk. He deserves everything he gets. Turn the bastard inside out."

He gestures with his hand.

"Go ahead—broke a lot of bones if you feel like it—put him in a coma while you're at it too—just make sure there are no witnesses to whatever you do when you pay him a visit."

He winces in pain and curses several times.

"I want him to suffer."

He nods several times.

"Yeah—that's exactly what I think he deserves. He made a mistake in coming after me—now it's time for payback."

Gary winces again and shakes his fist in anger.

"Make sure he's damaged beyond help."

He grins broadly and laughs.

"I know you guys don't ever give a damn what happens after you deal with someone who wronged you—that's how I feel about that scumbag Royer—I want him to pay for what he did to me today—and after you fix him I have someone else I want you guys to punish as well—name is Balfour—Susan Balfour."

He nods several times as he winces in pain yet again.

"That's right—she's no saint by any means."

He laughs.

"I got no problem with that idea."

He nods again.

14

"He's not here."

Alison Allington seems annoyed.

"I don't know where he is at this moment—he doesn't check with me every second. How many times do you need to hear Ben say he doesn't want anything to do with you until you believe it? Why don't you just leave him alone for now?"

Jacob Allington seems enraged.

"How dare you talk to me like that?"

Jacob clenches his fists.

"I'm warning you Allie—if you keep this attitude up toward me I'll get even—you'll regret dealing with me I assure you."

Alison looks at Jacobs curiously.

"Is that a threat?"

Jacob shakes his fist at Alison.

"I won't be denied access to my son—especially by my lousy ex-wife who never made an effort to know her place."

He looks at this car.

"You better change the way you talk to me."

He gets into his car and slams the door as Alison continues to stand in the driveway. As he starts the engine he looks out the window and angrily points his finger at her several times.

"Where does this Royer person live?"

Sergei Lycov wrings his hands.

"Did Barrington say?"

Kevin Kulkovich shoots Sergei a harsh look.

"I know where he lives."

Sergei wrings his hands nervously again and sighs.

"What happens after we pay Royer a visit?"

Kevin laughs.

"What do you think?"

He waves a pair of brass knuckles in the air.

"This dude will be seriously hurt when we leave. These brass knuckles are a punk's worst enemy—and this Royer dude is a punk—one that will have more than one broken bone in his body when we leave his pad. Then we pay the Balfour slut a visit and have fun with her. Barrington and Balfour must have had a falling out judging from his anger. I assume she double-crossed him over some deal or other. Nevertheless her fate is now in our hands and it's our job to teach her to respect our friends."

He laughs again.

"Barrington is one of us."

He smirks.

"Dude is really tight with Anton."

Sergei reacts.

"Where is Anton? Haven't seen him in weeks?"

Kevin shakes his head several times.

"He's at a corrections facility just outside of Santa Barbara last I heard. He was busted for breaking into some realtor dude's house. From what I was told he was wrapping up remaining business that Houghton Fawcett insisted be accomplished."

He sighs loudly and laughs.

"Levitov and his brother Alexei are really stupid. Alexei got busted for trying to break into a crypt back east and now his younger brother is locked up for breaking into a mansion."

He wipes sweat from his brow.

"Old man Fawcett dropped the ball too. From what I heard he went off his rocker rambling that some dead teenager was after him. Loren had his father committed to a hospital for loony tunes three weeks ago. Anton's lawyer has appealed his case several times but without much luck—Levitov is currently looking at serious hard time—probably San Quentin."

He looks at Sergei and rolls his eyes.

"There's been some talk online among his friends of a plan to break Levitov out of the facility he's being held at. Word has leaked that the Feds plan to move Levitov to an ultra-maximum security jail next month in Arizona. I might help in that endeavor if called to task—Levitov shouldn't be in jail for what he did. Stupid Feds just used the house-breaking incident to bust him since they didn't have anything else that would legally stick."

He slams his fist against the steering wheel.

"Once we free Levitov from jail the next step is finishing off everyone connected with that situation in New Orleans."

Sergei sighs loudly.

"Didn't CNN cover that story?"

Kevin nods.

"I assume—for a split second they followed it—but they apparently dropped the story—left it dangling—lost interest."

He wipes sweat from his brow again.

"Once we bust up Royer remind me to get some chow at some greasy spoon—I'm starved—got to fill my stomach."

He laughs loudly.

"Busting people gives me an appetite."

Sergei shakes his head in agreement and grins.

16

Sabrina glares at Lance Marler as he blocks her path on the sidewalk. He grins and seems ready for a fight. He sighs.

"I want you back."

Sabrina turns away.

"I have a boyfriend already."

Lance clenches his fist.

"That loser twerp isn't your boyfriend."

Sabrina takes a deep breath.

"He's more of a man than you'll ever be and everyone knows it—you're pathetic Lance—there is nothing you can do to change my mind about Jesse. I'm not coming back to you."

Lance grabs Sabrina's arm.

"You'll be with me or else—don't push me."

He twists her arm backwards and grins.

"If I can't have you neither will that frigging twerp."

He pushes Sabrina backwards.

"You're mine Sabrina—mine alone—and don't you forget it even for a second. I popped you and until I dump you we are still a couple as far as anyone is concerned. Get rid of Malinger or I swear I'll fuck him up so badly you won't recognize him when I'm through with using his face as a damn punching bag. I won't be insulted anymore—I own you—you're my fucking property."

Sabrina takes a step backwards.

"I'm going to talk to Colin Baxter about you."

Lance becomes enraged and angrily grabs Sabrina.

"You'll do no such thing."

He pulls her toward him and grins.

"If you do I'll kill you."

He grins as he sees her shocked reaction.

"Dump that twerp or else."

He leans forward and whispers in Sabrina's ear.

"I'm not joking about Malinger."

He presses his fist against her face and smirks slyly.

"You know I always do what I say."

He leers at her knowingly.

"I took your virginity in the backseat of my dad's jeep even though you begged me not to pop you on the night of your birthday party. But I took you down anyway—scored royally."

He forcibly tugs at her silk blouse and laughs.

"You and I need to get reacquainted."

He looks down at his swelling erection and grins.

"I think now is the perfect time for some backseat action between the two of us—I assume you're on the pill presently."

He pulls Sabrina closer to him.

"I'm in the mood no doubt—want a blowjob too."

Sabrina tries to push Lance away.

"This isn't happening."

He angrily twists her arm again.

"I say it is—my dick is getting impatient."

Sabrina spits his Lance's face. He reacts and releases his grip on her. She pushes him away as he wipes his face.

"Ask Racine Gilbert to spread her legs."

She backs away from Lance.

"You raped me that day."

He faces her.

"I did no such thing. I took what was mine. You were a tease and I'm the most popular jock in town who had already scored with just about every chick in Ocean Landing—what do you think would happen when we got together for a date? I had a rep for being with a lot of girls—and you were the only holdout I couldn't bed on my terms. I have rights in case you forgot."

He makes a lewd gesture with his finger.

"You wanted me as much as I wanted you."

He laughs loudly.

"I don't regret one moment."

He pulls out his cell phone and winks.

"Call Colin Baxter and tell him I raped you."

He makes a lewd gesture with his finger once more.

"He won't believe you—no one will."

He takes a step toward her.

"I want Malinger gone. You're done with him."

He takes another step forward.

"I expect the two of us to be back together shortly or I'll be forced to teach Malinger a painful lesson—it's up to you."

He looks at his cell phone again.

"I swear I'll hurt him—and it'll be your fault."

Sabrina looks at Lance oddly as he turns around.

"I mean it. I'll kill him and won't even care."
He watches her walk away.

17

"What are you going to do now?"
Paul Yarmouth looks at Cyril and shakes his head.
"What other choice do I have? Celine lied to me again. I should never have trusted her after what happened with Tyler."
He runs his fingers through his hair.

18

Jacob watches Ben walk down the street for a few seconds and then jumps out of his car. He runs toward Ben and stops.
"Ben?"
Ben turns around.
"We have to talk."
Ben seems annoyed.
"I don't want to talk to you."
Jacob becomes enraged.
"What did your mother say about me?"
Ben shrugs.
"I have eyes dad—I saw you and Susan Balfour coming out of a cheap motel on Spruce Street—you're a disgrace."
Jacob seems insulted.
"It wasn't what it looked like."
Ben shakes his head knowingly and turns away. Jacob watches Ben for a few seconds and faces his car again.

TO BE CONTINUED

A Brief Look at the Fourth Episode

Relationship issues from the past make a comeback for several people as a woman unable to let go of her failed marriage slips further and further down a path of no return while revenge leads to death for one person and an act of violence for another.

Twisted Reality

1

"He's something special no doubt."

Lana Collins turns away from the kitchen window and faces Larisa Lopez. She walks toward Larisa and grins broadly.

"Usually rich guys are pricks who think they're God's gift to women because they have tons of money to burn."

Larisa shakes her head.

"That's what I liked about him when we first met—he was so nice and real. He didn't have any of the usual hang-ups like most guys who inherited money. Maybe it was because he made his fortune by working hard and not having everything handed to him from the moment he was born like a lot of the guys I knew when I was at USC. Ward knows who he is and money hasn't changed how he sees the world—and it helps also that he's really good in bed—very charming and sensitive when need be."

She grins slyly.

"We're a very sexually active couple."

Lana rolls her eyes and sighs.

"I hate you—I really do."

She jabs Larisa several times.

"It's unfair you have a rich guy who's also good in bed."

Larisa laughs.

"I didn't plan it. But I'm glad we met."

Lana glances at the window again and shrugs.

"I've been with too many toads. There's no one here in Ocean Landing that I like—maybe I need to leave town like Sandra King did? She left town and found her Prince Charming in New York. They seemed so happy together when they visited a while back—I want what she has—what you have with Ward."

Larisa seems shocked at the statement.

"Scott Malone and Sandra met on a sinking yacht in the Virgin Islands and almost lost their lives. I met Ward by chance when he stopped by the inn the day he first arrived in Ocean Landing. It wasn't planned. We didn't get together until later. You can't plan something like that—it'll just end in disaster."

Lana shakes her head.

"I feel so alone at this moment."

Larisa makes a gesture with her hand.

"Don't be silly—you're not alone."

She walks over to Lana.

"You've got me and your parents. You've got your brother too—and your grandparents live just down the coast."

Lana shrugs again and sighs.

"I want a boyfriend."

She looks out the window once more.

"I'm tired of waiting."

Larisa reaches out to hug Lana.

"It'll happen when the time is right."

She looks at her watch.

"How about we go pay Karen Ewing a visit?"

Larisa gestures with her hand again.

"I heard Rebecca Martin is helping her out with the menu."

Lana smiles broadly and nods several times.

"No one cooks like her."

Larisa leads Lana toward the door.

"How about we put on a few pounds today?"
Lana grins and follows Larisa.

2

"How do I get a restraining order?"

Simon Andrews looks at Alison Allington curiously noticing the look of distress on her face. She sighs loudly.

"Jacob is at it again with his usual threats."

Simon leans back in his chair.

"If I bring Jacob in for questioning are you game to press charges if need be—it'll get nasty the minute he feels like he's being boxed into a corner—his lawyer will be all over you."

Alison shakes her head.

"I just want him to leave me and Ben alone."

Simon stands up.

"OK—I'll pay Jacob a visit."

They look at each other.

"But I can't promise anything."

Alison nods.

3

Sergei Lycov slams the door to his car and faces Kevin Kulkovich. He grins broadly as he looks at the apartment building. Kevin gives Sergei a knowing look as they begin walking across the street. They stop briefly and look around cautiously.

"Think that gorilla is expecting us?"

Kevin shrugs.

"Won't matter one way or the other as far as I'm concerned—the only thing that *does* matter is that Royer is going to be in a world of pain when we leave. Barrington said we could go rogue and I intend to do just that with this wretched fool."

They stand for a few seconds at the front door leading toward a small lobby. Kevin pulls out a pair of brass knuckles.

"This is gonna be fun—for us anyway."

He laughs and gives Sergei a knowing look.

"Like I said Royer is in for a world of serious hurt."

They enter the building seconds later.

<h1 style="text-align:center">4</h1>

Simon watches as Marlene Alderson comes toward him with a covered tray. He grins broadly and sighs loudly.

"Is that what I think it is?"

She nods.

"It is."

He leans forward.

"Sorry about lunch—I'm swamped."

Marlene waves her hand.

"Don't worry about it—thank Karen Ewing. She's so happy with how her diner is doing she gave me this tray for free."

Simon pulls the foil away and sighs again.

"I'm in heaven."

Marlene comes around the desk and they hug for a few seconds. She notices stacks of papers everywhere on top of Simon's desk. They face each other. She reaches out to stroke his cheek with her finger. He grins broadly as he grabs a piece of fried chicken from the tray. Marlene strokes his cheek again.

"You need to get away."

Simon laughs.

"I second that."

He gestures with his hand.

"I need you to tell Colin Baxter when you see him next."

Marlene glances at the room again and shrugs.

"Exactly where are Colin and David?"

Simon shrugs.

"Don't know. They were gone when I got here."

He rolls his eyes.

"Alison Allington stopped by."

Marlene gives Simon a knowing look.

"Let me guess—Jacob is up to no good—again."

Simon shakes his head.

"It seems for whatever reasons that jerk just can't get the message that his ex-wife and teenage son hate him."

He waves his hand.

"You'd think by now he'd see the light—but I guess he's still blaming Alison for all his terrible misfortunes of recent."

Simon scratches his beard.

"I think I may have to issue a temporary restraining order if he continues to play these kinds of stupid mind games."

Marlene seems confused.

"I thought Jacob had left town for good?"

Simon takes a bite of the fried chicken in his hand.

"He did—lives in Morro Bay."

He takes another bite.

"But if he goes near Alison again I'll have no choice."

He finishes off the piece of chicken.

"He's just making my job harder."

Marlene slides her fingers through Simon's hair.

"We've really got to get away."

She kisses Simon.

"This weekend if possible—even if it's just for a few hours up the coast where the two of us can enjoy sweet solitude."

Simon grins broadly.

"Is that your idea of a not-so-subtle hint that I need to spend more time in your bed—like tonight possibly?"

Marlene kisses Simon again.

"I miss having you next to me all night."

Simon sits up.

"Is that all?"

Marlene grins and nods several times.

"Uh-huh—that and I think we should get married."

Simon pulls Marlene toward him.

"What about my bad habits?"

Marlene playfully tousles Simon's hair and grins.

"I'll deal with them on a case-by-case basis."

Simon makes a lewd gesture with his finger and winks.

"I'll be a naughty husband."

Marlene leans over and kisses Simon.

"Is that a promise?"

Simon grins slyly.

"It is."

He looks at the stacks of papers.

"How are you doing? I've been so caught up in my misery I forgot to ask you how things were going with Louise Wong."

Marlene shrugs.

"Louise is fine—that whole ugly incident involving Nina Thurston a while ago shook her—but she's past it now."

Simon looks at the stacks of paperwork again.

"Nina's death along with that of Christopher Allington made for some pretty lurid headlines—Kyle Garland had a field day peddling endless *supposed stories* for weeks afterwards."

Marlene rolls her eyes.

"Don't get me started on Kyle Garland."

She tousles Simon's hair again.

"He gives new meaning to the word tabloid journalism."

Simon nods and pulls Marlene toward him.

5

"I don't want you in my life."

Jacob Allington angrily grabs his son by the arm and spins him around seemingly enraged. Without warning Ben Allington smashes his fist against his father's jaw. Jacob reacts and stumbles backwards. They look at each other for a few seconds as Jacob seems even more enraged than before. He sighs.

"How dare you hit me—I'm your father Ben—you owe me—show some respect you ungrateful son-of-a-bitch."

Ben rolls his eyes and turns away.

"In name only and nothing more—when was the last time you made a serious effort to behave like a real father."

Jacob recoils from the slight.

"I'm the only father you'll ever have."

He rubs his jaw for a few seconds.

"I won't tolerate your crappy attitude any longer."

Ben makes a lewd gesture with his finger.

"Fuck you."

He turns away and then stops.

"You should've thought about that before you cheated on my mother—she was right about you—you'll never change."

Jacob clenches his fists.

"That bitch mother of yours will pay dearly."

Ben spins around in a rage and lands another blow to Jacob's jaw. He falls backwards on the pavement as he watches Ben walk away. He pulls out his cell phone and begins dialing.

6
Los Angeles

"Is that all you can do?"

Leonard Masters slowly leans back in his chair as he stares blankly at Patrick Irvington. He runs his fingers through his hair as he seems lost for words. He leans forward and sighs loudly.

"That bastard Rolling is gunning for me."

Patrick shrugs.

"There's not much I can do. Our union can't overrule a state senator. He can remove you if he chooses to do so."

He sighs loudly.

"This thing with his brother won't just go away despite how it looks. His brother was a lowlife—but that said—Rolling is nothing of the sort—he can't be easily blackmailed."

Leonard smiles slyly.

"He's in politics—*there* has to be something. He must have taken at least one bribe—politicians are dirtier than cops."

Patrick takes a step closer.

"Rolling is clean—he has no dirt anywhere. If I were you I'd either get your act together and solve this case for Rolling or consider looking for a new job—there's no other way."

Leonard stands up and seems upset.

"A lot of help you turned out to be. I asked you to come over here to help me and instead you throw trash at me."

Patrick gestures with his hand.

"I don't know what you thought I could do—but there's no easy way out of this situation—none that's legal anyway."

Leonard shakes his head.

"Since when did the police union become respectable?"

He makes a lewd gesture with his finger.

"Like seriously? When did your tactics change?"

Patrick seems annoyed.

"I'm going to pretend I didn't hear what you just said."

He turns to leave.

"If I lose my job—I'm not going down alone."

Patrick turns to face Leonard again.

"Is that a threat?"

Leonard smirks.

"Take it anyway you like."

He walks over to where Patrick is standing.

"When Rolling came by initially he mentioned several high profile cases that the Los Angeles Police Department apparently looked the other way for whatever reasons. It would certainly be scandalous if somehow these files suddenly became public."

Patrick seems enraged as he stares at Leonard.

"I'm through talking to you."

He walks to the door and leaves. Leonard sighs.

"It's a mistake to fuck with me."

Leonard runs his fingers through his hair.

7

"Don't even think about scoring with her. That whore is someone else's property. A lowly runt like you need not apply."

Emerson Wilkerson watches as Mark Gilpin takes a step toward him. He glances briefly at Sabrina McCord and grins.

"You need to know your place in this town."

Mark aggressively pushes Emerson and laughs.

"One warning is all you'll get from me."
Without saying another word Mark walks away.

8

"This is terrific."
Lana takes another bite of her sandwich while Larisa watches people come and go from the counter nearby. She faces Lana and smiles slyly. She shakes her head several times.
"This place certainly has changed."
Larisa notices David Kipling sitting at the counter talking to Rebecca Martin. She turns back to face Lana and grins.
"David seems happy."
Lana glances at David and shrugs.
"That bitch Melissa played him for a fool."
She gestures with her hand.
"He's such a sweet guy—always respectable."
Larisa looks at Lana curiously.
"He's not seeing anyone."
She winks.
"He's got a nice body."
Lana shakes her head as Larisa grins again.
"I bet he looks really hot in a pair of tight boxer briefs—or in his birthday suit just out of the shower—dripping wet."
Lana rolls her eyes knowingly.
"Don't you get any ideas about matching me up with him—he's got too much emotional baggage from Melissa."
She glances at David again.
"She ruined him—her and Father William both. He's not gonna be much use to anyone for a while—a year probably."
Larisa gives Lana a knowing look.
"I think he'd make a nice date for next week."
Larisa winks at Lana.
"I bet he's quite the thrill in the sack."
Lana seems shocked at Larisa's statement.
"I'm not interested."

Larisa turns to look at David again as Rebecca hands him a package of food. She faces Lana again and smiles slyly.

9

"I'm so sorry your dad is a jerk."
Ben shrugs as he sits down next to Astrid Thomas.
"He's never going to change."
He runs his fingers through his hair.
"He made me so mad I hit him."
Astrid reacts.
"You hit your dad?"
Ben nods.
"He deserved it."
He sighs loudly.
"He's a lousy father."
He wipes sweat from his brow.
"His brother was no different if truth be known."
"I heard stories about your uncle."
Ben rolls his eyes.
"Uncle in name only—he never said two words to me my entire life. Every time he saw me in town he acted like I wasn't there. He was a prick. I'm not surprised at all he got iced."
Astrid looks at Ben curiously.
"Wasn't he killed by Father William?"
Ben gestures with his hand.
"Actually, I think he was taken out by the Russian mob despite what the news said. He and my father are mixed up with those guys—they play dirty when deals go bad—murder isn't something they tend to shy away from if they lose money."
He looks out at several stray cats eating from trays he placed earlier on several large rocks. He wrings his hands.
"My dad has never been there for me. He always had an excuse when I'd ask him to come to my baseball tryouts. I finally stopped asking. But cheating on my mother was the last straw as far as I was concerned—she didn't deserve what he did to her."

Astrid reaches out to hold Ben's hand.

"I love how sensitive you are."

Ben kisses Astrid lightly.

"I'll never do what my dad did."

They kiss again.

"He brought shame to my mother and I'll never forgive him for that—people were talking every day for a month."

Astrid shakes her head.

"How is it now with the talk?"

Ben looks at the stray cats once more.

"It's better now that my dad moved to Morro Bay."

He gestures with his hands again.

"If only he'd stay there and not come to Ocean Landing under the guise he wants to see me when in reality he's probably here for some shady dealings with his Russian contacts."

He makes a gagging gesture.

"Sometimes I dream that he isn't really my dad—and that I don't have a stigma attached to my last name because of things he and my worthless uncle did when they were children."

Astrid squeezes Ben's hand.

"My dad likes you."

Ben grins.

"I like your dad too."

He stands up.

"I wish he were my dad."

Astrid stands.

"But we'd brother and sister?"

Ben laughs.

"I didn't mean it that way."

They hug warmly.

"It's just that your dad cares about you. My dad couldn't care less how I feel. He cares more about enriching himself and sneaking around with hookers whom he calls girlfriends."

He looks out at the rocks in a distance.

"How about we go for a walk on the beach?"

Astrid seems pleased.

"How about we go away for the weekend?"

Travis Penwick pulls Carly Spellman toward him as they sit inside his car in a half-empty parking lot. He kisses her.

"You and me all alone in a hotel room up the coast."

Carly looks at Travis and grins broadly.

"Are you trying to tell me something sweetie?"

Travis smirks.

"Is it that obvious?"

Carly nods.

"You're like a pane of glass."

Travis laughs.

"I want some alone time with you—so shoot me already."

Carly slyly slides her fingers across his belt buckle.

"It's been almost a week."

Travis watches her fingers on the belt buckle.

"Uh-huh—it's been six days—*six days*—there's so much a guy can endure from his extremely beautiful girlfriend."

Carly tugs at his jeans again. He grins.

"Don't start something unless you plan to go all the way."

Carly kisses Travis.

"Is that what you want?"

Travis nods several times.

"Uh-huh."

Carly looks at her watch for a few seconds.

"We could go back to your place?"

Travis leans over and kisses Carly.

"I got plenty of condoms in the bathroom."

He grins broadly as he starts the engine of the car.

"Think your mother will miss you?"

Carly nods as they drive out of the parking lot.

"I have the afternoon off. She hired two extra people today—they're great at waiting tables from what I saw."

Travis leans over to kiss Carly again.

11

Rodney Royer falls against the sofa several times as he tries to stand up. He cries out in pain as Kevin and Sergei stand in front of him laughing as they continue to kick him. Bloody spots cover the floor as they lash out at him several more times. He cries out again and again but to no avail. Rodney looks up at Kevin and tries to pull himself up as Kevin violently kicks him in the face yet again. He grins as he sees Rodney's reaction.

"Let this be a lesson to you."

He kicks Rodney again.

"Fuck with our friends and you get fucked."

He kicks Rodney yet again.

"Next time you die."

He angrily rams his boot against Rodney's throat.

"Take heed."

They walk to the door. Rodney looks at them and begins snapping pictures using his cell phone. Kevin turns around in a rage. He pulls out his gun and look at Sergei for a second before walking over to where Rodney is lying. He casually places his gun against Rodney's temple and pulls the trigger without saying a word. Rodney dies instantly as his skull splits open. Kevin grabs the cell phone from Rodney's hand and smirks. He shrugs.

"He made me do it."

He begins to laugh as he faces Sergei.

"Dead men tell no tales."

He looks at the cell phone in his hand and smiles.

"This will never see the light of day."

Sergei nods and they leave the apartment. They pull the door shut and walk down the hallway toward the elevator.

12

Susan Balfour walks back and forth and looks at her cell phone. She turns to face Jacob standing in the doorway.

"Rodney isn't answering for some reason."

"Want me to go check on him?"

Susan shrugs.

"He's probably trying to pick up a new conquest at the bar down the street from his apartment. He's incorrigible."

Jacob closes the door behind him.

"I just had an encounter with my selfish son."

Susan rolls her eyes.

"That spoiled brat of yours needs a lesson in respect."

Jacob nods in agreement.

"His mother raised him wrong—made him a total wimp."

Susan walks over to Jacob and hugs him.

"Alison wasn't good enough for you."

Jacob laughs.

"Try telling her that."

He seems irritated.

"I gave her everything—and she thanks me by throwing me out of my own home and turning my son against me."

He clenches his fist.

"Ben needs to be taught a tough lesson."

He clenches his fist again.

"I've got to punish that boy—got to break his spirit."

He kisses Susan.

"He's been seeing Dexter's kid."

Susan rolls her eyes again.

"I know. I've seen them together all over town."

She makes a lewd gesture with her hand.

"Do you think Ben is fucking her?"

Jacob looks at Susan curiously and shakes his head.

"Why do you ask?"

Susan slides her fingers along Jacob's arm.

"What if he impregnates her?"

Jacob watches as Susan's fingers slide down to his pants and tug at the zipper. He grins broadly and gestures slyly.

"Is there a point to this—something useful?"

Susan slowly unzips the zipper to Jacob's pants.

Page 106 of 190

"Well, if your son got caught up in a scandal—it might split him and Dexter's kid up for good—it would also force him to come back to you and learn what it's like to be an Allington."

Jacob looks at Susan and smiles.

"You're one devious bitch without a doubt."

He laughs loudly.

"Cold and heartless too—but I like the way you think when it comes to revenge—especially if it means that brat of mine will be taught a lesson of respect when it comes to his father."

He glances at the bedroom door.

"I'm suddenly in the mood."

Susan gives him a knowing look.

"Tell me something I don't already know."

Jacob laughs loudly.

"We've been together for quite a while now. You started out with my brother and then you switched over to me when you realized I was so much better in bed—and now with Christopher six feet under I got you all to myself without competition."

He makes a lewd gesture with his finger.

"Of course there's that business with Jared."

He watches her reaction.

"How is that loser anyway?"

Susan wags her finger at Jacob.

"We're taking a break at the moment."

Jacob makes a lewd gesture with his finger again.

"Was it his choice or yours?"

Susan pushes Jacob toward her bedroom and laughs.

"That's for me to know and you to find out."

Jacob grabs Susan and kisses her passionately.

"Wycroft is a bore. He doesn't have a clue about how to treat a woman like you—kick him to the curb already."

Susan pretends to slap Jacob.

"This conversation is over."

Jacob pushes Susan against the wall.

"I think you should stop seeing other guys."

Susan pushes Jacob away.

"Are going to stop seeing other women?"

Jacob pulls Susan to him again.

"We're not talking about me—this is about you."

He looks down at his erection.

"This thing with Jared was a joke from the start—but I know you've been dallying with Gary Barrington recently."

Susan reacts as his erection presses against her thigh.

"I'm done with that jerk."

A smile spreads across Jacob's face.

13

Laura Stryker looks at an old newspaper clipping on the computer screen and sighs several times. She seems upset.

The Next Day

14

David Sherwood and Julie Cartwright sit across from Ward Brady at a picnic table under a large tree in Ward's backyard.

"How do you like Ocean Landing?"

David and Julie exchange a knowing glance.

"I like it—reminds me of the little town where I grew up."

Ward leans back in his chair and grins.

"That's what drew me to Ocean Landing—it has such a good vibe—I love small towns—especially seaside villages."

Julie looks back toward the house.

"I could see myself living here—instead of Los Angeles."

Ward takes a sip of coffee from his mug and looks at David for a few seconds. David notices but says nothing.

"Castle Beach must be steeped in colonial history. Lots of ancestors from the **Pilgrims**—there's enough drama there to fill volumes—starting with the events concerning the **Salem Witch Trials** in 1692—and ending with the **War of Independence**."

David nods in agreement and smiles broadly.

"Quite a bit—my relatives can trace our family back to the *Mayflower*. Almost everyone I know are related in some way or the other to **John Alden, Myles Standish, William Bradford** and **William Brewster** give or take a generation times twelve."

Ward smiles broadly.

"I love history—always have actually."

He smirks.

"I'm really nerdy about that sort of thing—even went as far as to visit Plymouth a few years back. It seemed so perfect except for winter—snow isn't my thing by any means."

David laughs nervously.

"I agree. I love New England—except at winter."

Julie jabs David and watches his reaction.

"David is majoring in film at UCLA."

Ward looks at David curiously.

"You plan to be a director?"

David shrugs.

"I'm contemplating it."

He looks at Julie.

"I'm also thinking about being a novelist."

Julie jabs David again.

"He could be the next **John Steinbeck**."

David seems uneasy.

"I'll settle for just being published."

Ward looks at David curiously.

"I actually own two small presses. One in California and one in New York—bought them last year at an open auction."

He takes a sip of coffee again and leans forward.

"Do you have anything ready?"

David shakes his head.

"Not really—just bits and pieces of stories."

He glances at the ocean in a distance.

"It's mostly just stories about my childhood."

He sighs loudly.

"Growing up in Castle Beach—dealing with peer pressure and weird stuff mostly—New England has lots of legends."

Ward grins broadly.

"Uh-huh—**Paul Revere**—I visited Boston too."

At that moment they see Larisa and Lana coming toward them from the house. Ward stands up as they approach.

15

Laird Cooke looks at his cell phone ringing as Cheryl Cooke shoots him a cautious look. He shrugs and sighs.

"I'm not ready to talk to him yet."

Cheryl rolls her eyes.

"His message earlier was clear."

She glances at Laird's cell phone again.

"He got Bastian Rego to draft a better script."

Laird waves his hand in the air.

"I don't care what he did—I don't want to do a horror film—I want to be taken seriously. **Jamie Lee Curtis** I'm not."

Cheryl watches as Laird heads to the door.

"I need some fresh air."

She looks at his cell phone lying on the sofa.

"Aren't you taking it with you?"

Laird shrugs.

"No."

He reaches for the doorknob. As he leaves Cheryl grabs the phone and begins dialing furiously. She looks at the door.

"You'll thank me later dear brother."

Second stick by and then the line is picked up.

"Yes—uh-huh—it's me Cheryl. I agree. We've got plenty to talk about concerning my brother. I think it would be smart to bring Bastian Rego with you to Ocean Landing tomorrow."

She nods several times and sighs loudly.

16

Lance Marler clenches his fists in anger as he sits in his car watching Jesse Malinger passionately kiss Sabrina goodbye.

"That smarmy bastard will really suffer at my hands when I get through with him—he's so dead—broken neck and all."

He watches Jesse go into the drugstore across the street.

"She is really pushing my last nerve."

He jumps out of his car and runs over to where Sabrina is standing with a cell phone in her hand. She seems shocked to see Lance standing in front of her. She slowly takes a few steps backwards as he approaches. He seems angrier than before.

"I thought I made myself clear that you were done with Malinger. He's yesterday's news. You and I have some stuff to get clear between us—starting with the backseat of my car."

He angrily grabs Sabrina by the arm.

"I'm not taking no for an answer."

Sabrina jerks free of his grip.

"Get lost Lance—I already told you we were done—leave me alone or I swear I'll have to report what you did to me."

Lance grabs Sabrina again and throws her against the wall of the parking lot. She seems stunned and gasps for air.

"It's no secret to anyone in town you lost your virginity to me—it's no big deal—everyone knows what a slut you are."

He laughs seeing her reaction.

"You wanted to be fucked by me—you begged."

Lance makes a lewd gesture with his finger and smirks.

"You're nothing but a damn cunt—plain and simple."

He twists her arm backwards.

"You're my whore Sabrina—and things are gonna change between us from today onward. I won't be derailed anymore."

Sabrina tries to push Lance away but he maintains his grip on her arm. He hits her across the face with his free arm.

"You *will* do as I say or else."

Lance seems ready to hit Sabrina again.

"I say differently."

Lance turns around to face Jesse and is met with several blows to his face. He lets go of Sabrina and falls to the pavement as Jesse lands several more blows to his head within seconds.

"If you come near Sabrina again I'll kill you."

Sabrina reacts to Jesse's words as he leads her away while Lance seems in a daze as he tries to stand. He watches Jesse and Sabrina leave the parking lot. He begins cursing loudly.

"You're a dead man Malinger—*dead*—do you hear me?"

They ignore him as he continues cursing at them. He wobbles for a few seconds as he tries to stand up. He sighs.

"I'm going to kill him—no doubt about it."

He begins laughing loudly.

"Once I rub that jerk out I'll have Sabrina back where I want her—in the backseat of my car—where she belongs."

He clenches his fists again in a rage.

17

Colin Baxter watches as Robert Widdemer covers the body of Rodney Royer and turns to face him. He sighs.

"Royer must have run afoul of the wrong people."

Colin seems confused.

"Are you saying what I think you're saying?"

Robert nods.

"It's a mob hit guaranteed."

He glances at the sheet-covered body again.

"I knew Rodney had shady friends—but not mobsters."

Colin wipes sweat from his brow.

"I think it's time we talk to some of his friends."

Robert hands Colin a small bag with a bullet inside. They look at each other briefly as Colin seems lost in thought.

"Royer's twin won't like this news one bit."

Robert shoots Colin a cautious look as he pulls out his cell phone. He suddenly grabs Colin by the arm. He sighs.

"I don't think this is the sort of news you deliver over the phone—might be better to go pay Wesley Royer a visit."

Colin shakes his head.

"Wesley Royer is in a mental hospital in San Francisco."

Robert looks at the sheet-covered body again.

"Uh-huh—I'm aware of that."

Colin shrugs and looks at the bullet inside the bag.

"I'm going to check this bullet out with my contact at the FBI and see what might shake loose—then I'll figure out how I'm going to deal with delivering bad news to Royer's brother."

Robert shoots Colin another cautious look.

"Don't say I didn't tell you so."

Colin rolls his eyes.

18

"This is getting to be really annoying."

Larisa glances at her cell phone and then faces her mother. Marta Lopez looks at Larisa curiously. She sighs.

"What's going on with your phone?"

Larisa shrugs.

"I'm not sure exactly—I've been getting a lot of strange calls for a couple of days now from some stupid teenager."

Marta shakes her head.

"Why would someone do that?"

Larisa rolls her eyes.

"Who knows—this world is full of kooks."

She sighs loudly.

"I've been resisting making a big deal about it but maybe it's time I deal with it headfirst—before it becomes an issue."

Marta shakes her head again.

"Did you tell Ward?"

Larisa nods.

"I did—he thinks I should report it sooner than later."

Marta gestures with her hand.

"I agree."

Larisa glances at the ocean.

"Lana is in a mood about not having a boyfriend."

Marta gives Larisa a knowing glance.

"Is this before or after you made an effort to fix her up with another loser—seems to me you'd better let her make her own choices when it comes to finding someone she likes."

Larisa glances at her cell phone.

"I just want to help."

Marta wags her finger at her daughter.

"Uh-huh."

She sighs loudly.

"Let her be."

Larisa snaps her fingers.

"Too late—I set her up with David Kipling."

Marta reacts.

"That poor man has been through so much already."

Larisa stands up.

"Lana is nothing like Melissa Barrow."

She makes a lewd gesture with her finger.

"Melissa was all wrong for David from the start. She had terrible rep in high school—slept with just about every straight guy in town—spent many weekends at abortion clinics."

Marta wags her finger at Larisa again.

"If this ends badly for Lana—she'll blame you."

Larisa ignores her mother and glances at the rocky cove below where several teenagers are hunting for something.

"Did you hear what I said?"

Larisa turns around and shrugs.

"Lana and I go way back—I'm not worried."

Marta shakes her head and seems worried as she watches her daughter. Larisa's cell phone begins ringing once more.

"Uh-huh—famous last words no doubt."

Larisa answers the phone.

19

Claire Brady looks at her cell phone and grins. She walks toward the small balcony of her hotel room. She sighs.

"I bet she's freaking out right now trying to figure out who's been calling her for the last few days and hanging up—bet she's told Ward about it too—hoping he'll be her hero."

Claire laughs and begins gesturing wildly.

"But it's all for nothing regardless—she's going to pay dearly for stealing my man—I intend to make her suffer."

She clasps her hand together.

"It's almost time to put my plan in motion."

She begins laughing again.

20

"Lance is really getting on my nerves."

Jesse clenches his fists as he and Sabrina walk along the surf as sprays of foamy water circle their feet. They stop and look out at the ocean as waves build in a distance. Sabrina turns around to look at the parking lot with a worried look.

"Marler has really gone off the deep end over seeing us together—if he comes near me again I'm going to report it."

Sabrina seems upset.

"I agree—not that it'll do a lot of good."

They look at each other.

"I was so hurt when he dumped me for Racine Gilbert—he laughed in my face when I told him I'd given him my virginity for nothing—said I was just a trick to him and nothing more."

She wipes a tear from her eye.

"He went around telling everyone I was easy while he was screwing Racine—then she got pregnant and he freaked."

Jesse looks at Sabrina curiously.

"Someone told me she had an abortion."

Sabrina shakes her head.

"Lance forced her to go to a clinic in Morro Bay even though she begged him not to force her end the pregnancy—said if she didn't get rid of their baby he'd take matters into his own hands and kill the baby himself. The day after she aborted their baby he dumped her and had sex with Marisa Walpole."

Jesse runs his fingers through his hair.

"I've met her at school a few times. She doesn't look like the type that would go for someone as scummy as Marler."

Sabrina shrugs and rolls her eyes.

"I never liked her. She was always sort of bitchy."
Jesse looks at Sabrina curiously.

21

"I didn't order a pizza."
The man seems annoyed as he looks at Susan and then at the two pizzas in his hand. He shoves it at her and sighs.
"I want my money, *bitch*."
Susan rolls her eyes.
"I didn't order anything and I'm not paying for it."
Kevin becomes enraged and shoves the boxes of pizza at Susan. She stumbles and he grabs her by the arm. He spins her around and laughs. He shuts the door seconds later and hits her several times. She screams as he hits her again. He laughs.
"I'm *so* going to enjoy you."
He laughs loudly.
"I like my whores feisty."
He hits her again as she tries to free herself from his grip which makes him even angrier as his fist crashes into her jaw.
"You and I are going to party."
At that moment the door to her apartment opens and Sergei stands in the doorway. He and Kevin share a sly glance as Susan realizes in horror what they have planned for her.
"You'll never get away with this."
Kevin laughs and forces her down on the sofa as he unzips his Levi's and pins her underneath him. He laughs again and turns around to look at Sergei standing a few feet away grinning.
"This bitch definitely needs to learn respect."
Susan cries out in shock as Kevin begins raping her.

22

"I need your help with a problem I'm having."
Lance looks at Mark and smirks. He angrily shakes his fist in the air and seems ready start fighting. He grimaces.

"Jesse Malinger."

Lance makes a slashing motion across his neck several times with his hand as Mark grins broadly and nods.

"It'll be really easy—we lure him to the beach and drown him in the surf—it'll be hard to prove anything afterwards."

Mark nods in agreement and laughs.

"Especially with the cops in this town—they're like the law in that old series *Dukes of Hazzard*. You know you're in trouble when farm hands have more brains than law enforcement."

They begin laughing loudly.

23

Wiley Wilkerson looks at the stacks of law books on his desk and sighs loudly. He turns around to look at his office.

"Starting over won't be as easy as I assumed it would be."

He runs his fingers through his hair and shrugs.

24

"Thank you—I appreciate it."

Simon nods as he watches Alison for a few seconds.

"Like I said before this might get nasty."

Alison nods and turns around to see Ben standing in the doorway watching her. She looks at Simon and nods again.

"I'm not going to back down. It's time I take a stand against Jacob—better late than never—enough is enough."

Ben comes toward his mother.

"What's going on? What did dad do?"

Simon and Alison look at each other and then face Ben again with a worried look. He notices and seems upset.

TO BE CONTINUED

A Brief Look at the Fifth Episode

Dangerous situations plague several people unwilling to let go of the past as reality begins to catch up to others with plenty of secrets—while several events begin to slowly unravel threatening the lives of more than just one person in Ocean Landing.

Episode 5
No One Would Tell

1

"Do you think this bitch learned a lesson?"

Sergei Lycov zips up his jeans and looks at Kevin Kulkovich with a sly grin. Kevin looks at Susan Balfour lying on the floor. She seems in shock. They begin to laugh.

"I doubt it—bet you anything she still thinks she's all that and more—thinks she's still got the world on a string."

He makes a lewd gesture with his finger.

"This bitch is in a class by herself—except for the fact she got played today—quite the trip without a doubt—nice."

He laughs again and gestures at her.

"Time to split—our work is done for now."

He walks over to Susan and pokes her with his feet.

"If you tell anyone—we'll be back for round two."

He kicks her in the chest.

"Do you understand?"

Susan nods several times amid tears as Sergei looks at his watch. He glances at Susan again once more. He sighs loudly.

"I think we should kill her."

Susan's eyes widen as Sergei walks over to where Kevin is standing. He looks down at Susan and smirks. Kevin shrugs.

"She's not a threat anymore—she's broken—damaged."

He laughs loudly and points at Susan.

"She was twice bested by two horny Russian guys."

He makes a lewd gesture with his finger again.

2

Claire Brady confidently looks at the gun in her hand and grins broadly as she casually plays with the trigger. She waves the gun in the air pretending to shoot. She begins laughing loudly.

"Her death will be just deserved."

She kisses the gun.

"She stole my man and now she must pay."

Claire kisses the gun again.

"Her tragic death will leave Ward free and clear to come back to me—come back and be a doting husband like before."

She smirks.

"I can't wait to see the pathetic look on her face when I pull the trigger and she realizes I've won—and she's lost."

She slides her fingers along the barrel.

"It'll be such a joyful moment."

She suddenly seems upset and looks at the gun again.

"Ward will thank me later."

She looks down at her stomach.

"He owes me."

She kisses the gun yet again and sighs loudly.

"He caused me to lose our baby when he took up with that whore and turned his back on me and our unborn baby."

She clenches her fist.

"It was all *her* fault I lost our baby."

She looks down at her stomach again.

"My baby died for *her* sins."

She slowly walks over toward the small kitchenette.

"I can't wait to kill her—to end her for good."

She begins laughing hysterically.

"Her screams will be like bells in my ears as she dies at my hand—I'll laugh in her face as she begs me to call for help."

She places the gun in a small box on top of the kitchen counter and closes the lid. She places the box in a drawer.

"Ward will be with me again soon—and then we can begin making babies together like we planned before he met *her*."

She clenches her fist again and sighs loudly.

"There's no other way."

She wipes sweat from her brow.

"It's either her or me."

She sighs loudly again.

3

Nancy Baker watches Cyril Spalding open the door for Sherilyn Matthews as they enter the diner. She seems upset.

"He's dating *her*?"

Jill Edmondson rolls her eyes.

"Why do you care?"

Nancy sighs loudly.

"I don't—but—but she's a virgin—*ugh*."

Jill glances at Cyril and Sherilyn as they sit down at the other end of the small diner. Jill turns to face Nancy again.

"You dumped him years ago."

Nancy seems annoyed.

"I dumped him after he lied endlessly to me."

Jill waves her hand in the air.

"Men lie—deal with it already Nancy."

Nancy glances at Cyril again.

"Ugh. What does he see in her?"

She turns to look at Cyril and Sherilyn again.

"She's looking for a husband—not someone like him to dally around with for a few months—doesn't he know that?"

Jill grabs Nancy's arm. They look at each other.

"Forget Cyril—you can do better."

Page 121 of 190

Nancy nods several times.

"I just wish he wasn't in my face all the time."

Jill snaps her fingers in front of Nancy's face several times.

"Hello—this is Ocean Landing—not Los Angeles."

She glances at Cyril once more.

"You'll see plenty—just ignore him already."

Jill pulls out a menu.

"He may be good-looking but he's empty upstairs."

She watches as Nancy smiles.

"Bedroom activity only lasts so long."

Nancy nods.

"It's just that I can't stand to see him enjoying life."

Jill rolls her eyes in frustration.

"No woman wants her ex to be happy."

She reaches out to gently touch Nancy's hand.

"When I broke up with Daniel I knew he was going to starting dating someone else eventually. But it was OK since he and I understood our situation. It just wasn't going to work."

Nancy looks over at Cyril again.

"I know what you're saying makes sense."

A movement at the front counter catches her eye as she sees Rebecca Martin and Karen Ewing talking. She sighs.

"Karen certainly is pleased with the turn of events in the last few days—this place is making bank without a doubt."

Jill turns to look at Rebecca and Karen.

"Carly is hardly ever around the diner anymore. I guess she found herself someone to spend her nights with now that she and Juan del Pino split after he slept with his trampy neighbor."

Nancy turns to look at Jill curiously.

4

Laura Stryker takes a sip of tea as she looks out at the ocean from a small pavilion overlooking the beach.

"This was one of my favorite places when I was a kid."

Enrique Lopez reaches out to stroke Laura's hair.

"I know exactly what you mean—it's like time stood still here and nothing ever changed despite it being over ten years so far. It looks exactly the same as it did when my folks bought this place and reopened for business all those years ago."

Laura turns to face Enrique.

"The last few months have been really therapeutic for me. Living here again has brought back so many memories from the past and laid bare the pain I felt when my family was forced to sell the inn and leave town. But it's really changed my perspective in ways I never thought—things are different now for me."

Enrique slides his hand into Laura's hand and grins.

"I hope I had something to do with that."

Laura leans over to kiss Enrique.

"Absolutely—you've been my rock throughout all the pain I had to work through when I came back seriously unsure if I was doing the right thing. You're the most wonderful boyfriend a woman like me could ask for—sensitive and kind—perfect."

Enrique kisses Laura again.

"I've never met anyone like you before."

Laura pulls away.

"What do you mean by that?"

Enrique shrugs.

"It's hard to explain."

He sighs.

"You hardly ever talk about your life other than when you lived in Ocean Landing—there's so much I don't know."

Laura seems upset and stands up.

"There's not much to know."

She looks out at the ocean again.

"I told you about Solvang. Then I lived in Los Angeles for a while when I was in college. My life has been quite boring."

Enrique stands.

"Didn't you have boyfriends?"

Laura sees nervous as she faces Enrique.

"Of course I did—several. But none ever worked out the way I'd have liked—too many problems to work through."

Enrique seems confused.

"What about me?"

Laura faces Enrique.

"So far so good—I like you."

He smiles.

5

"Did you hear what I said?"

Todd Zimmer turns to look at Dorothea Wong.

"Of course I did."

He sighs.

"You told me you met Laird Cooke. Said he was really nice to you—and that—and that he told you he was vacationing."

Dorothea gestures as they sit at a picnic table facing the ocean. Todd grins as he lazily shuffles his feet in the sand.

"Why would someone as famous as Laird Cooke ever come to a loser town like Ocean Landing for a vacation?"

He points his finger at Dorothea.

"Unless he did something really bad and he's hiding from the press—I heard those Hollywood types are always doing stuff that causes their careers to take a tumble when the truth is exposed in those sleazy tabloids you see at the supermarket."

Dorothea wags her finger at Todd.

"You've been watching too much *TMZ*."

Todd grins.

"Guilty as charged."

He faces Dorothea and seems bothered by something.

"I got accepted at Stanford—with Alan's help."

Dorothea reacts.

"My little brother is the best."

Todd nods in agreement.

"I'm still thinking about it—nothing definite."

He wipes sweat from his brow.

"Ocean Landing Community College is OK—but I really think Stanford is my ticket out of having limited chances."

They look at each other.

"Alan says Stanford is really cool."

He wipes sweat from his brow once more.

"He's majoring in political science."

Dorothea seems confused.

"What about Serena and the baby?"

Todd winces.

"I haven't told her yet."

Dorothea shakes her head.

"This isn't something you can casually ignore."

Todd runs his fingers through his hair.

"Like I said earlier I'm still thinking about it—nothing has been decided yet either way. I haven't told my folks either."

Dorothea looks back at the parking lot.

"This seems like a serious recipe for disaster."

Todd reacts to the comment.

6

Los Angeles

"I don't like playing games with selfish actors."

Jeffrey Webber rolls his eyes as he gets into his car and slams the door loudly. He watches as Bastian Rego continues to stand next to the car. He seems upset. Jeffrey sighs loudly.

"The film company clearly wants Laird Cooke to do this picture and stated publicly that they wouldn't go forward with any other name actor. He has clout—plain and simple."

Bastian shrugs and gets into Jeffrey's car.

"This is highly insulting—Cooke is nothing special as far as I'm concerned. I admit I wanted him initially—but his prima donna antics have seriously pissed on my enthusiasm—truth."

Jeffrey waves his hand in the air.

"He'll come round—his sister said he just wanted a better script—said he didn't want to do the same thing over and over again because he'd get typecast as a B movie actor. From that point of view I have to admit I can understand his fears."

Bastian shoots Jeffrey a harsh look.

"Who does he think is? **Tom Hiddleston**?"

Jeffrey sighs.

"He could be if he gets the opportunity."

Bastian rolls his eyes in mock contempt as he looks at Jeffrey for a few seconds. He quickly pulls out his cell phone.

"I need a backup plan."

Jeffrey reaches out to grab Bastian's arm.

"Who are you calling?"

Bastian pulls his arm free of Jeffrey's grip.

"Jared Isling."

Jeffrey reacts.

"I really don't think that's a good idea Bastian."

Bastian gestures with his hand.

"Jared Isling is a team player."

Jeffrey drives out of the parking lot.

"He was—but he creates scandal wherever he goes. He was my client for a while—but he wouldn't play nice in public."

Jeffrey sighs loudly again.

"He has a disdain for the press—ever since he got *outed* he has been looking for a fight. I tried to work with him for a while but he refused to focus on the bigger picture. I even snagged him a role in the movie about that *incident* that took place in the Caribbean a few months back. But he messed that up royally."

Bastian leans back and sighs.

"Oh—that's right I remember. He picked a fight with Scott Malone at a premiere in Westwood—Malone slugged him."

Jeffrey sighs loudly once more.

"I had to drop him after that incident. Malone's boss Roland Parker threatened to sue—Isling hasn't worked since."

Bastian puts his cell phone away.

"OK—OK—let's see what Laird Cooke has to say before we look for a replacement—but I'm not promising you."

Jeffrey grins broadly.

"I understand completely."

They notice the San Diego Freeway up ahead.

7

Susan begins to cry softly as she looks at herself in the mirror. Her clothes are torn and red welts crisscross her arms and legs. She slides her hand between her thighs and winces.

"Oh God—did this really happen to me?"

She leans against the sink.

"Why?"

She looks at herself in the mirror again.

"I can't tell anyone about this—they warned me."

She sighs loudly.

"No one can know what happened."

She walks over to the shower.

"I've got to forget this ever happened."

She sighs again.

"They seemed to know me for some strange reason."

She steps into the shower and stops.

"What am I going to do?"

She reaches for the faucet.

8

Colin Baxter slowly leans back in his chair and stares at Simon Andrews standing in front of his desk. He shrugs.

"Royer's death was quite brutal. Haven't ever seen someone so busted up in Ocean Landing—terrible way to go."

He gestures with his hand and sighs.

"He was worked over pretty good before being shot at close range in the head. Royer must have done someone wrong in a big way no doubt—probably ran up some gambling debts."

Simon shakes his head and sits at the edge of the desk.

"Royer was without question not too bright a guy—but I never knew him to have an affinity for gambling. He wasn't into that scene from what I heard. He liked bars and women."

Colin glances at the open file on his desk.

"Maybe one of those women he liked so much had a jealous boyfriend that wasn't pleased when he found out Royer was slamming his girl on the sly—would make sense if that was what took place—Susan Balfour comes to mind right away."

Simon nods in agreement.

"Uh-huh—her guy fits the bill perfectly."

Colin jumps up.

"Time we pay him a visit."

Simon follows Colin out the door seconds later.

9

Laura waves to Enrique as she gets into her car. As she drives away she waves again. She turns onto the main road and slows down. She sighs loudly and then begins to cry loudly.

"This is so hard."

She pulls over to the side of the road.

"He's so nice—so trusting."

She wipes tears from her eyes.

"I don't deserve him."

She wipes another tear from her eye.

"Why should I do?"

She looks at the road in front of her and sighs.

10

"I can't believe you did that."

Laird Cooke angrily looks at his sister as she waves her cell phone in her hand. She walks over to where he's standing.

"Someone had to be the adult in the room."

Laird shoots Cheryl Cooke another harsh stare.

"I thought I made it clear I was through doing crappy horror movies just to make Jeffrey a huge ton of money."

Cheryl rolls her eyes.

"I told him there would be conditions."

Laird looks at Cheryl suspiciously.

"It's not too late for me to find a new manager."

Cheryl laughs and points at her brother.

"Go ahead if you feel like it."

She turns away.

"I've been thinking of retiring anyway."

Laird faces Cheryl.

"You're thinking of quitting on me after all we've been through together? I thought you liked being my manager?"

Cheryl nods.

"I could be persuaded."

Laird shakes his head and sighs.

"Uh-huh—seems like you're playing me."

Cheryl walks over to where Laird is standing.

"It's time to get real about Bastian."

Laird rolls his eyes.

"I'm not doing another horror movie."

He sighs loudly.

"I'll quit acting first."

Cheryl grabs Laird by the arm.

"No need to act rash little brother—stupid decisions can have long-lasting effects—Bastian Rego won't play nice."

Laird pulls away from Cheryl.

"I'm tired of playing childish games."

He clenches his fist.

"*I'm done.*"

He looks at his cell phone lying on the sofa.

"Call Jeffrey and tell him I'm done. Tell him he can go fuck himself—go find another loser to represent. I've had it."

Cheryl seems upset.

"I'll do no such thing—especially now."

Laird walks over to the sofa.

"Then I'll do it myself. I think it's time Jeffrey know I'm not his lapdog anymore. I'm tired of acting anyway. I want to be normal again—have a life without photographers following me everywhere I go like I'm some sort of freak or something."

Cheryl rushes over to Laird and grabs his cell phone.

"When Jeffrey gets here we'll talk about all your concerns about what movies you want to do. I promise he'll listen to what you have to say—and if he won't then I'll go along with you."

Laird shakes his head several times.

"I want to do movies about real people who beat the odds despite having everything stacked against them. A movie like A Street Cat Named Bob would be perfect. That's the type of film I want to do—not that garbage that Jeffrey keeps sending me."

Cheryl seems confused.

"Wasn't that the movie about a stray cat that helped a drug addict from London get clean—turned his life around?"

"The trailer is on YouTube."

He grins.

"Want to see it?"

Cheryl watches Laird as he turns on his computer and begins feverishly searching YouTube. She shakes her head.

"I don't think a movie like that is your thing."

Laird turns to face Cheryl.

"How would you know Cheryl? All you've ever done is go along with Jeffrey's game. I saw the movie when it came out and then read the book. **Bob the Cat** changed the life of **James Bowen** and showed what someone is truly capable of when they have hope. **Luke Treadaway** was excellent playing James."

Cheryl watches as the trailer begins playing.

"I still don't think."

Laird glares at Cheryl coldly.

"I'm not going to bend anymore."

He sighs loudly.

"I want to do better movies."

He turns his computer off.

"I don't mind if I have to do TV in order to get better work than Jeffrey has been getting me—but something has to change or I'm done with Hollywood—done with pretending I'm happy when I'm not. I've done this too long and I want a change."

Cheryl wrings her hands.

"I don't like you hanging out with Lance."
Gina Bertinelli pulls Mark Gilpin toward her.
"He gives me the creeps."
Mark laughs.
"Lance is a good guy—he's just intense."
Gina shrugs.
"He's really weird. I've heard stories from Sabrina about how controlling he was when they dated. He scared her."
Mark rolls his eyes.
"Sabrina's a tease—and she lies too."
Gina pushes Mark away.
"I'm going to pretend you didn't just say that."
Mark laughs loudly.
"Sabrina is just mad because Lance popped her and then threw her over for Racine Gilbert—nothing but sour grapes."
Gina seems upset as she stands.
"Is that how you see it?"
Mark nods.
"How else can I see it?"
He grins.
"Lance popped her and then got bored."
He laughs slyly.
"It happens all the time."
He stands.
"I popped Veronica Cabot last year at the prom and then hooked up with her cousin Marlisa Evans the next day."
Gina seems aghast at Mark's comment.
"Is that how you see me?"
Mark makes a lewd gesture with his finger.
"Stop making a big deal already. You girls know how we guys think. Sex is a necessity for a high school guy before he heads off to college. Bagging as many girls before graduation is important to someone like me and Lance. I had a rep before we started dating. I've never tried to hide who I've been."

Gina takes a step away from Mark.

"Exactly how many girls have you slept with?"

Mark laughs loudly again.

"I have no idea—I've lost count—what's the big deal."

Gina shakes her head.

"I think I'm going to be sick."

Mark winks at Gina.

"I thought you knew I was playing even when we began dating—knew I was sleeping with other girls regularly."

Gina reacts.

"I thought we were exclusive."

Mark makes a lewd gesture with his finger again.

"You thought wrong."

Gina sighs loudly.

"We're through."

Gina turns away. He smirks slyly.

"Suit yourself."

Gina doesn't turn around.

12

"I think your uncle is really cool."

David Sherwood grins broadly as he steps out of his car and runs his fingers through his hair. He seems pleased.

"His girlfriend digs me too."

Julie Cartwright slides her hand around David's waist.

"You seem pretty sure of yourself."

David laughs as he leans over to kiss Julie.

"I'm a charming guy—deal already."

Julie tugs at his belt.

"You're quite the charmer in bed too."

David gestures with his hand.

"Without a doubt—but I'm quite charming in other areas too. Your uncle and his girlfriend were really into what I had to say earlier about my views on things I experienced as a kid."

Julie looks at David curiously.

"Exactly what did you mean when you told my uncle what happened to you in Castle Beach was impossible to explain?"

David shrugs. He lowers his voice.

"I can't explain what happened—so how can someone else who didn't witness what I did explain it? What happened still seems like it was all a bad dream. One day everything was fine and then my friends and I were facing a scary nightmare."

He looks away.

"Maybe one day I'll understand it—understand what I saw was real and not something that only happens in novels."

David sighs loudly.

13

"I already told you I don't know anything."

Colin and Simon look at each other and at Susan. They notice her disheveled appearance as she tries to close the door of her apartment in their faces. Simon glances at Colin again.

"Are you all right?"

Susan seems irritated.

"I'm fine—never better—I just want to be alone."

She tries to close the door again.

"I don't know why Rodney was murdered."

She sighs.

"He and I weren't that close."

Colin and Simon look at each other.

"That's not the impression I got from you earlier."

Susan rolls her eyes and shrugs.

"Go away—please go away."

Simon gives Colin a cautious look.

"A man was murdered—quite brutally I might add—I think you know something—and if you were involved—well."

Susan seems about to cry.

"I didn't kill Rodney—I had nothing to do with it. Please just leave me alone. I want to be by myself right now. OK?"

Simon notices the bruises on her arms.

"How did you get those bruises on your arms Susan?"
Susan glances at her hands.
"I fell. I'm clumsy."
Simon shoots Colin a suspicious look.

14

"Ugh—I hate her."
Racine Gilbert makes a gagging gesture.
"Gina Bertinelli thinks she's better than everyone else."
Mark nods and pulls Racine toward him.
"I'm done with her."
He smirks.
"If she wants to go through senior year at Ocean Landing High without a boyfriend that's her deal—I've got to be me."
He grins broadly.
"She's just as stuck up as Sabrina McCord."
Racine rolls her eyes.
"Ugh—I hate Sabrina even more than I hate Gina."
She makes a gagging gesture again.
"Lance was so nice to her—he made her popular and how does she repay him? She dumps him for that geeky freak from San Diego. What's so special about Jesse Malinger anyway?"
Mark makes a slashing gesture across his neck.
"His days are numbered."
Racine looks at him curiously.
"What does that mean?"
Mark laughs and kisses Racine.
"Let's just say that **Tom Holland** wanabee is in for some choppy seas. Malinger has a really nasty surprise coming."
He laughs again and gestures with his hand.
"Lance wants Sabrina back between his legs and doesn't care what he has to do to get her to see things his way. She royally insulted him by taking up with Malinger and he's out for blood no doubt—Malinger's blood to be exact. Kid is doomed."
Mark laughs and kisses Racine again.

"Sabrina and Gina should be more like you. Lance and I have had so much fun since you transferred to Landing High from Larkspur Prep. Gina especially needs to stop being so snooty. We're both gonna miss you when we head off to college."

Racine slides her fingers across Mark's lips.

"We've got several months yet."

Racine grins slyly.

"It would be such a shame if word got out that you impregnated Gina. She would be a freak show all over town once the rumor got underway—people would point and laugh."

Mark shakes his head.

"We only did the deed a few times."

Racine laughs.

"One time is all it takes."

Racine makes a lewd gesture with her finger.

"It would serve her right."

Mark smirks.

"She'd probably want to kill herself."

Racine makes a lewd gesture with her finger again.

"The scandal would be brutal."

Racine begins to unzip Mark's jeans.

"Where is your car parked?"

Mark grins and points to the parking lot.

"Place is practically empty."

Racine tugs at the zipper and smirks.

"I assume you have a stash of condoms in the glove compartment? Condoms are a real deal breaker with me."

Mark waves his hand in the air.

"I always come prepared."

Racine winks.

"I can't decide who I like better—you or Lance."

Mark grabs Racine's hand and leads her toward the parking lot a few feet away. He turns to face her and grins.

"I'm better without a doubt—banged more girls than Lance. Popped plenty virgins—slept with a few mothers also."

He makes a lewd gesture with his finger.

15

"How did you get this number?"

Ward Brady slowly walks across the lawn in his backyard as he continues talking. He seems upset and sighs loudly.

"I thought I made myself clear about our marriage."

He stops suddenly.

"We're done Claire—our divorce is going through the motions—I think you should start facing reality for a change."

Loud yelling can be heard on the other end.

"I'm not changing my mind."

He looks at his cell phone and shrugs.

"It's not Larisa's fault. You killed our marriage."

He runs his fingers through his hair.

"Please don't call me again."

Screams can be heard coming from the cell phone.

"There's nothing more to say."

He hangs up.

"Who was that?"

Ward turns to see Larisa Lopez looking at him from a few feet away. He runs his fingers through his hair again and sighs.

"Who do you think?"

Larisa seems upset.

"How did she get your phone number?"

Ward shrugs.

"I have no idea."

He sighs loudly.

"She was really upset."

Larisa reaches where Ward is standing.

"Claire just refuses to accept our marriage is over."

Larisa reacts.

"Is she still in San Francisco?"

Ward looks at his cell phone and shrugs.

"I don't know."

Larisa looks at Ward nervously.

16
Los Angeles

"This thing is getting out of hand."

Patrick Irvington leans back in his chair as he looks at Edward Rolling. He glances at a stack of folders on his desk.

"Masters is out for blood."

Edward shakes his head and sighs.

"How is this mess my fault?"

Patrick leans forward.

"Masters is threatening to release large volumes of files on unsolved murders from way back when. This sort of thing could create a scandal of which the likes have never been seen."

Edward shakes his head.

"That's between you and Masters."

He turns to leave and stops.

"I want my brother's murder solved."

He notices Patrick's reaction.

"If Masters can't do it—find someone who can. Find someone soon—I'm not a patient man. Stop dawdling around."

Patrick makes a gesture with his hand.

"It's not that easy."

Edward seems annoyed.

"I think it is."

He looks at his watch and sighs loudly.

"My brother's murderer is out there somewhere—I want them found and brought to justice—or else a lot of people are going to be really unhappy with the outcome—namely you."

He walks to the door and turns around.

"I want results—I'm done with excuses—someone knows something. Find them and do what you guys do best when it comes to finding answers even in impossible situations."

Patrick seems insulted.

"I don't think I like what you're implying."

Edward smirks.

"Do I look like I care one way or the other?"

He seems annoyed as he slowly reaches for the doorknob.

"I'll expect an answer shortly."

He leaves without waiting for an answer.

Two Days Later

17

"What do you mean she doesn't know where Laird might be? He knew we were coming—his rudeness is insulting."

Jeffrey shakes his head and looks at his cell phone again and then at Bastian. He slowly walks over to Bastian.

"Cheryl said he just up and left. He didn't say a word."

Bastian seems ready to explode.

"That was two days ago."

"I know."

He looks at his cell phone again.

"She said she's checking hotels in the area."

Bastian wrings his hand.

"I'm losing patience with his behavior."

He sighs loudly.

"No one treats me like this."

He grabs his jacket from the sofa nearby.

"He better show his face in the next several hours or I'm leaving. I've had it with his attitude. He's not the only actor in demand at the moment—*he* can be replaced quite easily."

Jeffrey nods in agreement.

"I certainly understand."

He watches as Bastian storms out of the hotel room.

"The clock is ticking."

Jeffrey nods as Bastian slams the door shut. He throws his hands in the air. He seems stressed out as he sighs loudly.

"I guess it's time I tear up his contract. His career is over before he really made a difference—made a serious impact."

He slowly walks to the balcony.

"Who knew an actor with so few credits would have such a massive ego? So many would kill for the chances he's had—today certainly hasn't gone well by any means. I think it's time I call his sister and deliver the bad news—before it leaks to the press."

He grabs his cell phone and begins dialing.

18

"That was your sister."

Simon turns around to face Laird.

"She said Bastian is royally pissed. He's threatening to deep-six your career over your behavior. She said Jeffrey is freaking out too—said he was really worried for you."

Laird rolls his eyes.

"Jeffrey is greedy. He'll do anything to make a quick buck from his clients. I'm done with him—done with the games."

Simon seems upset.

"Maybe you should tell him?"

Laird shakes his head.

"What for—he just wants to hear I'm going to do Bastian's stupid movie. I've been raked over the coals long enough."

He sighs loudly.

"I got into acting because I wanted to do good work."

He waves his hand in the air.

"But it didn't turn out the way I thought."

He stands up.

"I signed with Jeffrey when my first agent died in a plane crash—believing he would send me out for good roles. But he lied and instead sent me out on auditions for one horror movie after another. Like seriously, how many times can I do movies where people get stabbed or hacked to death by some crazy freak?"

He begins to laugh.

"I want to focus on material that means something. Even Cheryl bought into Jeffrey's game—I've just had enough."

Laird runs his fingers through his hair.

"There's just so much one person can take."

"I'm fine with you hanging out at my pad but you can't stay here forever. You haven't left my place for two days."

Laird reacts.

"I'm OK."

Simon walks over to Laird.

"Face this Bastian person and tell him to shove it."

Laird slaps Simon on the back.

"Easy for you to say buddy—Bastian is extremely cruel when he doesn't get his way—revenge is a way of life for him."

He wrings his hands.

"He enjoys destroying people's lives."

Simon seems confused.

"Want me to speak to him?"

Laird shrugs.

"No."

He slowly walks toward the kitchen.

"I think I know what I have to do."

Simon turns to look at Laird. He seems confused.

19

Gary Barrington grins broadly as he shakes hands with Kevin and Sergei. He turns to look at the highway up ahead. He watches them as they get into Kevin's car. He sighs loudly.

"Thanks again for what you did for me."

Kevin smirks.

"It was our pleasure."

Sergei laughs.

"That Balfour chick threw quite a party."

Gary makes a lewd gesture with his finger and smirks.

"She had to be taught a lesson."

Kevin and Sergei exchange looks.

"We've got some business in Los Angeles to attend to but don't think anything of it if you need our assistance again."

Gary nods in agreement.

20

Jacob Allington watches Dexter Thomas for a few seconds before he jumps out of his car and runs toward the driveway.

"Dexter Thomas."

Dexter turns around and sees Jacob standing a few feet away with clenched fists. Jacob takes a step forward.

"You and I have to talk."

Dexter rolls his eyes.

"We have nothing to talk about."

Jacob seems about to explode at any second.

"I say differently."

Dexter looks back at his house and shrugs.

"I want you off my property."

Jacob waves his clenched fist in the air.

"I'll bust you up good—just like when we were kids."

Dexter looks back at his house again.

"If I recall it was actually Christopher that used me for target practice—but oops—he's dead—killed by a serial killer."

Jacob reacts.

"How dare you."

Dexter grins broadly.

"He got what he deserved. No one in Ocean Landing would disagree. In fact I bet there's plenty people overjoyed."

Jacob loses control and takes a swing at Dexter but misses and seems unprepared when Dexter slams him hard with several punches. Jacob falls backwards and seems in a daze.

"Get off my property."

Jacob glares at Dexter for a few seconds before he notices Astrid Thomas and his son looking at him from the driveway.

"You'll pay for this Thomas."

Ben Allington seems upset as his father pulls himself up. Jacob shakes his fist at Dexter in anger as he slowly stands.

"You'll be sorry you ever messed with me."

Dexter ignores Jacob and walks over to where Astrid and Ben are standing. They watch as Jacob slowly drives away.

Page **141** of **190**

Nancy looks at Greg Williams as he places a lid on a cup of coffee he just bought from a nearby coffee shop. He turns to face her and notices she seems upset as they begin walking.

"What did I do now?"

Nancy shrugs.

"You didn't do anything. I'm just in a mood."

Greg grins broadly.

"What did my brother do?"

Nancy rolls her eyes.

"It's Cyril."

Greg gestures with his hand.

"I thought you two were finished ages ago."

Nancy jabs Greg.

"He's going out with Sherilyn Matthews."

Greg takes a sip of coffee.

"So?"

Nancy jabs Greg again.

"I thought Cyril and I had something special going—then he dumped me without so much as to why. It's been hard."

Greg laughs.

"Cyril isn't anything special—let it go."

Nancy sighs loudly.

"I just don't want him dating Sherilyn Matthews."

Greg takes another sip of coffee.

"You just don't want him to be happy because he dumped you and moved on right away—just be honest already."

Nancy seems upset as she wipes a tear from her eye.

"Cyril knew I loved him."

Greg looks at the cup of coffee for a second.

"I think the bigger question is did he feel the same way about you? Nope—I think not knowing Cyril as well as I do."

Nancy's eyes suddenly flashes with anger.

"I don't recall asking you for your crummy advice."

Greg gestures with his hand and laughs.

"I say it as I see it. Take stock—Cyril has moved on with someone new—maybe it's time you did the same. It can't hurt to mingle a bit until you shed Cyril for good from your heart."

Nancy shakes her fist at Greg.

"When did you suddenly become smart?"

Greg begins laughing.

22
Los Angeles

"I know who killed your brother."

The man turns to face the street and seems nervous as he listens to the voice on the other end. He sighs several times.

"Uh-huh—that's right."

He nods several times and shrugs.

"I think we need to meet."

He watches several people walk by.

"Uh-huh—I understand."

He nervously looks at the pay phone.

"Two o'clock tomorrow at Brand Park in Glendale."

He nods several times.

"I know what you look like."

Mason Crumble hangs up the phone and faces the street for a few seconds before he begins walking down the sidewalk.

TO BE CONTINUED

A Brief Look at the Sixth Episode

The personal lives of multiple townspeople fall under scrutiny as nothing appears to be what it seems—while events that refuse to remain forgotten create chaos among many—as two persons with grudges plot to destroy their rivals once and for all.

Episode 6
That Secret Sunday

1

"I want answers and I want them now."

Wesley Royer stares coldly at Colin Baxter as he stands up. Colin stands and sighs loudly. He seems upset and shrugs.

"Like I told you when we spoke initially—we have nothing to go on—the place was swept clean and came up empty."

Wesley angrily clenches his fists.

"I want my brother's killer found or else."

Colin gestures with his hand.

"We're doing the best we can at the moment."

Wesley turns around.

"My brother didn't deserve to be killed like a dog on the street—he was a good guy—everyone in town liked him."

Colin runs his fingers through his hair.

"I'll keep you updated."

Wesley takes a step forward.

"Oh, I think you'll do more than that Baxter. I won't wait around until you decide to do your job—I want results."

He takes another step forward and points at Colin.

"I'm good friends with Kyle Garland. He and I go way back. He would certainly love to tackle a story like this no doubt."

Colin shakes his head in disgust.

"Talk to Kyle Garland if it makes you feel better."

He runs his fingers through his hair again.

"But it won't change anything. We've got nothing."

Wesley glares at Colin for a second or two and then bolts from the room. Colin turns around to face David Kipling.

"How the hell did he get out of that loony bin up north?"

David seems confused and shrugs.

2

"One shot—that's all it'll take to end her."

Claire Brady giggles as she glances at the box lying next to her as she drives along the road. She begins to laugh.

"Her death will make things right."

She slows down as she reaches the driveway in front of a huge house shaded by several trees. She stifles a laugh.

3

Bastian Rego gets into a taxi and gives Jeffrey Webber an odd look before he pulls the door shut. Jeffrey sighs loudly as he watches the taxi drive away and turns to face Cheryl Cooke.

"Laird just ended his career in Hollywood."

Cheryl nods.

"I'm afraid you're right."

Jeffrey seems upset.

"I still might be able to help."

Cheryl looks at Jeffrey curiously.

"But Bastian just left in a huff—he's pissed."

Jeffrey waves his hand.

"He is—but the studio might be able to sway him to taking a pause—at least until they figure out what Laird is up to."

He looks back at the entrance of the hotel.

"**Marilyn Monroe** played this game back in the day and she got everything she wanted—at least for a while anyway."

Cheryl shakes her head.

"Didn't they replace her with **Jayne Mansfield**—changed the game completely. Monroe's career suffered terribly."

Jeffrey rolls his eyes and shrugs.

"Your brother better get his act together."

Cheryl looks at her cell phone again.

4

Cyril Spalding grins as he looks at Sherilyn Matthews from across the table. He reaches out to touch her hand gently.

"Last night wasn't so bad—was it?"

Sherilyn smiles broadly.

"You were the perfect gentleman."

Cyril smirks.

"I'm a man of my word. I told you I want something different than I've had lately. I'm tired of playing the field."

He sighs loudly.

"I've failed miserably at the endeavor."

Sherilyn seems upset.

"Every woman in town has stories about you."

Cyril winces and leans back in his chair.

"That was the old me Sherilyn—jumping from bed to bed with every woman I met at Winkle's Bar wasn't the real me."

He strokes her fingers lightly.

"I'm really trying to change my ways."

Sherilyn pulls her hand away.

"I like you Cyril—you're really good on the eyes."

She looks around the diner.

"But I'm not sleeping with you until I know it's going somewhere. I'm not the type of girl that plays silly games."

Cyril smirks and taps his fingers on the table.

"I appreciate you being honest with me and I agree."

He leans forward and grins slyly.

"I can wait until you feel the time is right."

She nods and notices Karen Ewing walking toward her.

5

"What would you say if I stayed here?"

Simon Andrews turns around to look at Laird Cooke with a shocked reaction on his face. Laird glances at the cell phone in his hand briefly and walks over to where Simon is standing.

"I could get my own place."

Simon shakes his head.

"You're serious about this? Moving to Ocean Landing?"

Laird nods several times.

"Would that be OK with you?"

Simon takes a sip of coffee from a mug nearby.

"It's up to you."

He sighs loudly.

"Do you really think you can actually give up your career after how hard you worked to establish yourself in Hollywood?"

Laird bites into the bagel in his hand.

"What career? Bastian Rego will make good on his threat to totally destroy me. No one will want to work with me."

He grimaces.

"That jerk has ruined many careers already just because he thinks he can do whatever he wants. Jeffrey and my sister are terrified of him—and he knows it. I'm ready for a change."

Laird looks at his watch.

"I think Ocean Landing would be the perfect place to get away from it all. People seem nice here. Not much drama."

Simon begins laughing.

"Is that so? *Peyton Place* has nothing on Ocean Landing."

He slowly runs his fingers through his hair.

"This town has its share of oddball characters."

Laird takes another bite of his bagel and sighs loudly.

"It can't be worse than Hollywood."

Simon rolls his eyes.

"We'll see about that."
Laird looks at Simon curiously.

6

"I don't want to date David Kipling."
Lana Collins seems slightly annoyed as Larisa Lopez smiles broadly with glee. She leans toward Lana and whispers.
"He hasn't dated anyone since Melissa's death."
Lana rolls her eyes knowingly.
"I'm not going out with him tonight."
Larisa smirks.
"Oh yes you are—you can't back out now."
Lana looks out toward the ocean.
"He's a complete mess—no woman wants him."
Larisa shakes her head.
"David Kipling isn't messed up. He hasn't dated anyone because he doesn't think anyone will go out with him."
Lana sighs loudly.
"I can't deal with the drama Melissa inflicted on him."
Larisa reaches out to pat Lana's hand.
"Who said you had to deal with what Melissa did—it's a date—not a therapy session—David is not a complainer."
Lana leans back in her chair.
"If this turns out to be a disaster I'll never forgive you."
"David Kipling is a wonderful guy."
Lana waves her hand in the air.
"So says you."
At that moment they are both shocked to see Claire standing a few feet away from them with a gun in her hand.
"I love a party—don't you?"
Claire begins laughing as she takes a step closer.
"Time's up *bitch*—I'm here to take back what's mine."
Larisa watches as Claire comes closer waving the gun in her hand. Lana seems frozen in shock as Claire laughs again.
"He belongs to *me*—not *you*."

Claire glances at the gun again and then faces Lana.

"The question is what should I do with you?"

She looks at the gun once more.

"Ward is mine—he belongs to me—and me alone—and once I kill you I'll have him back—back in my bed and my life. He and I will make another baby together—to replace the one you caused me to lose when you began sleeping with my husband."

Lana seems confused as she looks at Larisa.

"Who is this *person*?"

Claire becomes enraged and angrily slams the barrel of the gun against Lana's face causing Lana to fall backwards.

"I'm Ward's wife—who the hell are you? How dare you talk to me like that? Exactly what are you doing here anyway?"

She points the gun at Larisa and smirks.

"You must pay for your sins."

Larisa seems unable to move as she watches Claire's finger fiddling with the trigger. She sighs loudly as Lana tries to stand up. Claire spins around and points her gun at Lana.

"I think I'll kill you first."

She begins laughing hysterically.

7

"He has no idea what's about to happen."

Lance Marler grins broadly as he turns to face Mark Gilpin sitting next to him inside his car. They smile as they watch Jesse Malinger drives out of the gas station and head onto the street.

"He thinks he's going to meet Sabrina."

Lance laughs slyly.

"Stupid dummy doesn't realize it was *me* who texted him not Sabrina. He's so dead—Pinnacle Point is the perfect place to teach that fool a lesson he won't forget—place is isolated."

Mark fist bumps Lance and nods in agreement.

"I predict you and Sabrina will be back together before the end of the week—she'll fall back in line without a doubt."

Lance laughs loudly.

"She and I have so much time to make up for after the way she insulted me by hooking up with that pathetic twerp."

He slams his fist against the steering wheel.

"I can't wait to kill that fucker."

He slams his fist against the steering wheel again.

"I want him dead—he shamed my reputation in front of everyone in town by going out with my girl behind my back."

Mark seems amused by Lance's anger.

"What about your deal with Racine Gilbert?"

Lance shrugs.

"What about her?"

Mark gestures with his hand.

"There's plenty bad blood between Sabrina and Racine after you slept with Racine right after you hooked up with Sabrina that first time. Sabrina has had it out for Racine ever since."

Lance shrugs again.

"What about it?"

He notices Jesse leaving the main highway and heading down the narrow road leading to Pinnacle Point. He grins.

"I hope he begs for mercy."

Mark jabs Lance.

"You're one sick dude."

Lance clenches his fist and shakes it in the air.

"He needs to pay for what he did."

He looks at Jesse's car up ahead on the narrow road.

"Sabrina was mine before he came to town."

He grimaces.

"There's no other way."

They watch as Jesse pulls over near a clump of trees and jumps out of his car. Lance slows down and watches from afar.

"Won't he be surprised when he figures it out?"

Jesse begins nimbly climbing along several large rocks that lead to the sandy beach below. Lance and Mark grin as they step out of Lance's car. Lance snaps his fingers and smirks.

"His neck will break like a frigging twig."

Mark nods as they quickly head toward the rocks.

8

Karen watches as Cyril walks toward the bathroom and faces Sherilyn. She looks around cautiously several times.

"I'm glad to see you out and about—but I'm sure you're aware of Cyril's history. He's been around quite a bit."

Sherilyn shakes her head.

"I'm fully aware of his history."

Karen looks around again.

"I just don't want to see you get hurt."

Sherilyn nods.

"Thank you."

She leans forward and whispers.

"He knows he's on thin ice until he proves himself."

Karen smiles broadly.

"I'm glad."

She notices Cyril coming toward them.

9

"No one will care when they find you dead."

Claire grins broadly as she looks at the gun in her hand.

"No one ever cares about husband-stealing whores."

She laughs hysterically.

"I warned you to stay away from Ward."

She takes a step closer to Larisa.

"But you didn't listen—did you? You continued sleeping with him even though you knew he was my husband."

Claire looks at the gun and laughs again.

"Ward told you over and over again how much he loved me but you didn't care—you toyed with his affections."

Larisa notices a movement at the edge of the backyard.

"Used his body—begged him to impregnate you—made him believe you loved him—but it was all a lie. I'm the *only* one who ever loved Ward. I'm the only one who understands him."

From the path leading to the backyard Ward Brady stops cold in his tracks as he sees Claire standing in front of Larisa waving a gun back and forth. He runs toward Claire in a panic but stumbles. Claire turns to face Ward. Her rage increases.

"You're not supposed to be here."

She turns to face Larisa again.

"She has to die—that's the only way for us to be together after what she did. She killed our unborn baby—ruined me."

Ward looks at Claire in shock.

"What are you talking about Claire?"

Claire faces Ward.

"This bitch made you cheat on me—caused me to lose our unborn child—broke up our marriage like a common slut."

Ward looks at Larisa and then at Claire.

"She did nothing of the sort. *You* destroyed our marriage not Larisa. *You* cheated on me—killed my trust in you."

Claire looks at the gun in her hand.

"No—it's all lies Ward—it was you—not me. I never cheated on you—not from the day we began dating. I couldn't cheat on you even if I wanted to. You mean the world to me."

Her eyes fill with tears.

"You were the one who *cheated* on me with *her*. She used you—made you believe she loved you. Tempted you with her body and turned you against me—she did it all—not me."

Lana and Larisa look at each other silently.

"She has to die."

Ward takes a step forward.

"Give me the gun Claire."

Claire shakes her head and faces Larisa.

"I have to kill her."

Ward sighs loudly.

"Give me the gun Claire."

She takes another step toward Larisa and in a flurry of movement Ward rushes her. They struggle with the gun as Larisa and Lana spring into action trying to help subdue Claire.

10

"I could've told you that."

Cynthia Rodgers rolls her eyes as she faces Jacob Allington. He seems angry as he slowly walks over to where she's standing at the mini bar in her living room. He sighs loudly.

"That punk son of mine is seriously disgracing the Allington name by hanging out with the daughter of Dexter Thomas of all people. You should've seen it—Dexter out in his yard acting like my son was his property. It was disgusting."

He wipes sweat from his brow.

"I'm going to teach him a lesson he won't forget."

Cynthia hands Jacob a glass of wine.

"What do you have in mind?"

Jacob looks at the glass of wine in his hand.

"I'm not sure yet."

Cynthia smiles slyly

"I might be able to help."

Jacob looks at Cynthia curiously.

"Do tell."

Cynthia slides her hand around Jacob's waist.

"How about we talk about it later?"

Her hands slide down to his jeans. She grins broadly.

"I think you need to work off some frustration."

A grin spreads across Jacob's face.

"I like how you think."

She leads him toward the hallway.

11

Jesse walks about the narrow beach looking around. He shrugs and turns toward the rocks. Not far away he notices Lance and Mark making their way toward him. He looks around.

"What the fuck are they doing here?"

Lance grins broadly and calls out to Jesse.

"You and I have to talk."

Jesse seems confused and looks at Mark noticing his weird grin as they come closer. Jesse takes a step backwards.

"There's no place to run."

Lance winks at Mark as they continue to walk toward Jesse. Waves crash on the rocky surf not far away. Jesse glances at the rocks behind Lance and Mark. He sighs loudly.

"I see that the two of you are sharing a brain again."

Lance reacts.

"I'm gonna break you."

He lunges at Jesse.

"Get him."

Mark watches with glee as they fall on the beach and begin punching each other. Jesse suddenly maneuvers himself on top of Lance as the surf crashes around them. Several times he dunks Lance under the water. Mark stands a few feet away egging Lance onward—but it does little good as Jesse continues to hit Lance multiple times in the face as he yells for help. Mark finally intervenes but Jesse lays him out with one kick to the groin and he falls against some nearby rocks. Jesse stands up.

"Next time know your opponent before you attempt something as stupid as this—oh—by the way in San Diego I was close friends with several gang members—best damn fighters in the world—excellent teachers too. Have a nice day dick wad."

He walks away as Lance cries out in pain.

12
Washington DC

"I don't see how I can help."

Maxwell Pendergraft leans back in his chair and sighs.

"I'm familiar with the case but it was handled from the Los Angeles office. I agree that there are a lot of things in the Dennis Bosley case that remains unanswered—at least for now."

He rubs his chin several times.

"I'll do some checking but I can't promise anything."

He stands up and walks around.

"I'll call you tomorrow morning."

He nods several times as he walks to the door.

13

Jill Edmondson looks at her cell phone briefly and slowly turns to face Carter Benning. He waves his hand in the air.

"Well? What did the FBI say?"

Jill shrugs.

"They said they'd check back with me tomorrow."

Carter seems confused.

"I thought you said your lead at the FBI in Los Angeles stated this guy was one of the best—said he'd be able to link the missing pieces together on Dennis Bosley's background."

Jill reacts and sighs loudly.

"Maybe she was wrong about his abilities—I think they might have hooked up previously from the way she acted—it might have clouded her judgment—he sounded hot actually."

She looks at her cell phone again.

"This Dennis Bosley thing is getting more and more curious as the days tick by. For a guy with a rap sheet a mile long it seems there's hardly anything to be found on his life before he came to Ocean Landing. It's almost as if Dennis Bosley didn't exist at all before he assumed the identity of Father William."

Carter walks over to where Jill is standing.

"What about Bosley's wife?"

Jill rolls her eyes.

"Nothing—she's as much a mystery as Bosley was to the FBI—no records can be found about her life before her marriage and subsequent murder at the hands of her sicko husband."

Carter pats Jill on the shoulder.

"You'll figure out. I have faith in you."

Jill nods as Carter walks to the door. He stops.

"I'm going to pay Colin Baxter a visit to follow up on the death of Rodney Royer—his brother is royally freaked out."

Jill watches Carter leave. She sighs loudly.

14

"Oh my God—what have you done?"

Blood is everywhere as Ward seems in shock as he looks at Claire. She glances at the gun in her hands and faces Lana and Larisa. They slowly back away from her as she circles them.

"I'm going to kill you both."

Claire raises the gun as Lana looks at the back entrance of the house and screams. Claire turns around and at that moment Lana hits her with a potted plant. Claire falls backwards as Larisa looks at Lana. Seconds later she runs toward Ward as he gasps for air. Lana begins dialing furiously on her cell phone. Not far away Claire groans as she comes to. Lana notices and grabs the gun lying a few feet away. She points it at Claire as Larisa holds her hand over the wound in Ward's chest. She seems in a panic.

15

Jacob kisses Cynthia passionately as he reaches for the doorknob. She smiles slyly and hugs him. They laugh.

"I'm feeling much better now."

Cynthia grins broadly.

"That was the idea."

They kiss again.

"There's still that matter with that punk son of mine. He needs to be taught a lesson—that boy's a disgrace to me."

Cynthia looks at Jacob curiously.

"Better leave your ex-wife out of it—a restraining order is nothing to play with Jacob—she's playing hard no doubt."

Jacob clenches his fists.

"I can't believe she did that."

He grits his teeth.

"She's dragging my good name down the drain. Telling lies about me—making people believe horrible things."

Cynthia winks and kisses Jacob.

"Maybe there's a way to get back at her without being so obvious—I'd be glad to help—Alison and I have history."

Jacobs nods in agreement.

"Oh, that's right—you took her boyfriend away from her on prom night—had sex with him if I recall—in Alison's car."

Cynthia laughs and kisses Jacob again.

"He was really good looking—wanted so badly to fuck me that night—so I let him—was it my fault that she caught us?"

Jacob kisses Cynthia again.

"That was some catfight if I recall."

Cynthia makes a lewd gesture with her finger.

"I've never regretted it."

She laughs slyly.

"Wesley Royer was worth it."

Jacob rolls his eyes.

"He also slept with his stepmother."

Cynthia kisses Jacob again.

"Do I detect a glint of jealousy?"

Jacob begins to laugh.

16

Larisa and Lana seem in shock as Marta Lopez reaches out to hug her daughter. Simon leans against the wall in the hallway talking on his cell phone. Seconds later he comes toward Larisa and Lana. They turn around to face him. A few feet away Marta notices Colin shaking his head and looking at his cell phone.

"Claire has been placed under suicide watch."

Larisa sighs loudly and shrugs.

"She totally lost it—ranting and raving like a lunatic."

Simon nods and turns to look at Colin.

"What did her psychiatrist say?"

Colin looks at Larisa and then at Simon.

"Claire Brady is mentally ill."

Lana rolls her eyes.

"You think?"

Several doctors and nurses rush by.
"How is Ward doing?"
Larisa seems about to cry.
"He's still in surgery."
At that moment they see a surgeon slowly coming toward them. Everyone turns to face him. Marta hugs Larisa again.

17

"He's not right for you."
Nancy Baker seems upset as she faces Sherilyn.
"He's a cheater."
Sherilyn rolls her eyes.
"Get a life already."
Nancy grabs Sherilyn by the arm.
"He used me—cheated on me barely two weeks into our relationship and refused to apologize. He's a pathetic loser."
Sherilyn pulls free of Nancy's grip.
"I know all about Cyril's rep. He told me you two were not getting along—said you were mean to him—so he cheated."
Nancy seems stung by the comment.
"He's a liar."
Sherilyn sighs loudly and walks away.
"Sounds like pot calling the kettle black to me."
Nancy turns to see Helene Jeffreys standing behind her. Her eyes are icy cold. She seems angry. Nancy sighs.
"What do you want?"
Helene glances at the front door of the diner.
"It seems to me on numerous occasions I've seen you with both of the Williams brothers—bedding them no doubt."
Nancy reacts to the slight.
"How dare you."
Helene smirks.
"The truth will set you free."
They stare at each for a few tense seconds.
"You best mind your own business."

Page 159 of 190

Helene laughs and gestures at Nancy.

"Or what—what are you going to do if I don't stay out of your business? You haven't changed one bit since college."

Nancy grins slyly.

"Should I tell everyone about you and Father William?"

Helene reacts.

"What about Father William and me?"

Nancy makes a lewd gesture with her finger.

"You lost your virginity to him."

Helene glares at Nancy.

"Father William is dead—old news—but what about you."

Helene looks at the front door of the diner.

"It would be so sad if word got out about you and Larisa's father. Terrible scandal for sure if his children knew their father was having rough sex with one of their former classmates."

"You're a bitch Helene—no wonder you can't get a man in your bed even if you paid—disgusting troll—*ugh*—freak."

Helene watches as Nancy bolts for the door. She smiles broadly as she turns to see Carly Spellman looking at her.

"What was that about?"

Helene waves her hand in the air.

"I have no idea—Nancy Baker is probably on drugs or something. She was acting irrational—seemed buzzed."

Carly watches as Helene walks to the front door of the diner and leaves. Carly shakes her head several times.

18

Malcolm Brady hugs Larisa warmly for a few moments. He turns around to look at the others and then at the hallway.

"I got here as soon as I could. How's Ward? Is there any word on how he's doing? Did one of the doctors say?"

Larisa seems upset.

"No word yet—he's still in the operating room. No one has said anything. I feel like I'm walking on pins and needles."

"He'll be OK. Ward is a fighter."

Malcolm lovingly embraces his parents Andrew Brady and Diana Ordway. He glances at his stepfather Lloyd Ordway and turns to face Julie Cartwright and David Sherwood. Julie hugs Malcolm and David offers his hand to shake. Malcolm sighs.

"Is there anything I can do?"

Larisa shakes her head.

"Where's Claire?"

Lana rolls her eyes.

"She's in the mental ward where she belongs."

She glances at Larisa.

19

"That fucking punk got lucky."

Lance rubs his jaw as he climbs the rocks leading to the road up ahead. Behind him Mark remains silent as he follows Lance. They reach the road seconds later and look around.

"I should've brought my dad's gun."

He laughs.

"It would've been so easy to blow him away."

Mark makes a gesture with his hand.

"He won. Deal with it already."

Lance seems irritated by Mark's comment and sighs.

"He won the battle—but I'll win the war."

He clenches his fist.

"I'm going to make him pay."

He stops.

"One bullet and it's all over for that jerk."

He laughs.

"Sabrina will belong to me again—no doubt about it once I rub that twerp out—she'll fall in line and I'll own her soul."

They walk over to where his car is parked.

"I think I'll pay Jesse a visit tomorrow."

Mark rolls his eyes.

"Tomorrow is Sunday?"

Lance makes a lewd gesture with his finger.

"I'll wait until his mother leaves for work and then I'll do what needs to be done when it comes to that punk. When she comes home she'll find his corpse with a bullet in his head."

He laughs loudly as Mark shakes his head.

"Sabrina will have no choice but to come back to me—on my terms no doubt—she'll beg me to forgive her for being so rude and I'll tell her I'll think about it after she spreads her legs."

Mark grins broadly and nods.

20

"She did what?"

Sherilyn leans over to kiss Cyril.

"She said you were no good—said you cheated."

Cyril seems upset.

"I was no saint by any means when it comes to being in stable relationships—but she was anything but pleasant."

He sighs loudly.

"She treated me like I was her property."

He looks at Sherilyn.

"I never felt like we were in a real relationship so I started looking elsewhere after the first few days. It just happened."

He leans back on the sofa.

"She always seemed so negative no matter how much I tried and then it didn't matter anymore. I wanted her out of my life as quickly as possible. I know she still wants me back."

He runs his fingers through his hair.

"I took up with Susan Balfour knowing how much Nancy detested her. She caught us together and freaked out."

He rolls his eyes.

"She kept saying how much she loved me."

He pulls Sherilyn toward him.

"She refused to let go."

They kiss.

"I heard she began spending time with Daniel Williams and then traded him for his brother—that didn't last either."

Sherilyn tousles Cyril's hair.

"Nancy has always been a bitch—thinks everyone owes her something—plays nice until she gets what she wants."

Cyril kisses Sherilyn again.

"Susan and I parted ways soon after and I fooled around with Jill Edmondson briefly and then began dating Jennifer Slater a few weeks later. She and Nancy have a lot in common."

Sherilyn rolls her eyes knowingly.

"Tell me about it—Jennifer is certifiable."

Cyril stretches out on the sofa.

"I'm certainly chosen my share of problem women."

Sherilyn tousles Cyril's hair again.

"A man should never encounter such problems in his quest to find himself a good partner—it's just so wrong."

Cyril nods several times.

"Uh-huh—I second that view without a doubt."

Sherilyn notices his erection straining under his Levi's. She reaches out to touch the outline of his penis as he sighs loudly.

"I think I've made you wait long enough."

She takes his hand and glances at the hallway.

21
Los Angeles

Edward Rolling looks at the images as they flash across the screen. He turns to look at Mason Crumble and sighs.

"Her picture is here somewhere?"

Mason nods in agreement.

"I cover most of the stories pertaining to the Los Angeles and San Diego areas. I clearly remembered talking to her."

He runs his fingers through his hair.

"She was really nervous when I spoke with her about your brother's death. She seemed scared actually. Claimed she barely knew him. I thought she was quite odd—freaky almost."

Edward looks at the computer screen again. He shrugs.

"There are thousands of images here."

Mason shakes his head.

"I didn't say it would be easy. Online databases aren't exactly good at separating material the way we'd like."

Edward turns to look at Mason again.

22

Rebecca Martin watches as April Estes cautiously enters the diner. She seems upset to see her. She rolls her eyes.

"You'd think she'd know better."

Karen notices and gives Rebecca a curious look.

"She's learned from her mistakes."

Karen sighs loudly.

"I'm sure she regrets dealing with Father William—she almost became one of his victims. She was incredibly lucky."

Rebecca notices several people whispering.

"That depends on how you see it."

Karen turns to look where Rebecca is looking.

23

Larisa looks up just as Charles Benning comes toward them. He seems stoic in his appearance. Larisa stands.

"Is he?"

The doctor looks at her and nods.

"He's in recovery."

Larisa breathes a sigh of relief and faces the others.

"Can I see him?"

"You can—but only for a few minutes. He needs to rest. He's been through quite a ride—will certainly have quite a story to tell the grandkids when he's old and gray—and in a rocker."

She turns to face Ward's parents.

"Do you?"

They both wave their hands in the air.

"You go first—tell him we're waiting outside."

Larisa smiles weakly and follows Charles.

"Who the hell does she think she is?"

Nancy angrily slams her keys down on the counter as she walks into the kitchen. She stops and looks at the door.

"That frigid bitch needs to mind her own business before she goes about telling other people how to live their lives."

Jill pours herself a glass of wine and sighs.

"Forget about Helene Jeffreys."

Nancy faces Jill.

"I'd like to. I'd like to throw her off the bluffs at Larkspur Point right now. I really hate her. No wonder she can't land a man. Who would want such a judgmental bitch in their bed?"

Jill stands and walks over to Nancy.

"Let me guess—is this really about Cyril."

Nancy gestures with her hand.

"Why is he dating Sherilyn Matthews of all people? Like seriously what does she know about men? She's a frigging virgin damn her—saving herself for the *right* man. Get me a fucking barf bag—like as if there's such a person to be found. Ugh."

Jill sighs loudly.

"Let it go already."

She puts her arms around Nancy.

"What about Patrick Woods? He's single."

Nancy shakes her head.

"He came out as gay last week. I heard he cheated on Carly's friend Sabine with Raphael—the flower shop owner."

Jill rolls her eyes knowingly.

"Oops—I didn't see that coming—I guess him wearing leather all the time should've been a glaring hint—oh my."

Nancy gives Jill an odd look and pulls away.

"I just don't want to see Cyril happy. He needs to pay for using me the way he did. He decided to break up but didn't say anything until I caught him in bed with Susan Balfour."

Jill seems upset and faces Nancy.

"Cyril and I fooled around after you slept with Daniel and then with Greg. It happened only once. I didn't plan it."

Nancy turns around to face Jill. She seems in shock.

25

"Out of the kitchen this minute or else."

Marlene Alderson watches Simon as he turns around to face her. He seems confused. She walks over to him.

"I'm not kidding."

Simon grins.

"What happens if I refuse?"

Marlene takes him by the hand and leads him toward a sofa in the living room. He watches her curiously and grins.

"I want to help you make dinner."

Marlene kisses Simon.

"You worked plenty hard today already."

She kisses him again.

"There was more drama today than there was on *Dallas*."

Simon gestures with his hand and smirks.

"It wasn't that bad—medium drama actually."

Marlene walks back into the kitchen.

"Uh-huh."

She faces him.

"You're going to relax and enjoy some peace and quiet for a change—just deal already—at least for the next hour or so."

Simon grins broadly.

"You're up to something—aren't you?"

Marlene wags her finger and begins laughing.

"Whatever gives you that idea?"

Simon stretches out on the sofa and smirks.

"I must be in serious trouble. You're treating me with kid gloves. Is my life in danger—should I be terribly worried?"

Marlene walks over to where Simon is sitting and grins.

"Uh-huh—I'd be worried if I were you."

Simon begins to laugh.

"Is that how you're going to play this game?"
Marlene smirks.
"Uh-huh—keep you guessing."
Simon makes a lewd gesture with his finger.
"I'll defend myself if need be."
Marlene walks back toward the kitchen.
"It won't do you any good."

Simon grins as he watches her place a covered tray into the oven. He begins to whistle happily. Marlene smiles as she turns to look at Simon again. He notices and smirks slyly.

26

"He actually sent you a fake text?"
Jesse nods as Sabrina McCord wipes dried blood from his face. He winces several times as she swabs him. He sighs.
"Marler has totally lost it."
He sighs again.
"He thinks he's in some TV show or something."
He rolls his eyes.
"It was weird—he and Mark seemed totally out of it. Like they actually thought I would just stand there and do nothing as they tried to bust me up like a ragdoll. Of course what they thought and what transpired were two different things."
Sabrina faces Jesse.
"I think you should report what they did."
Jesse waves his hand in the air.
"They'll just deny everything. There were no witnesses anywhere around—unless someone else was on the beach."
Sabrina reaches out to swab Jesse's bruises again.
"Lance is dangerous. He's certifiable."
Jesse looks at Sabrina curiously.
"What exactly happened between you two?"
Sabrina seems about to cry and turns away from Jesse.
"He's not who I thought he was—he *used* me."
She seems about to cry and sighs.

"I think Natalie knows about us."

Hardy Wheeler laughs as he pulls April toward him.

"And your point would be?"

April kisses Hardy.

"She's a friend of mine—I don't want to hurt her."

Hardy laughs.

"Too late—the minute you unzipped my jeans and dared me to fuck you in the supermarket bathroom the deal was off concerning your friendship with Natalie. You took what you wanted and didn't give a rat's ass about Natalie's feelings."

April pushes Hardy away.

"It's your fault actually if you must know."

Hardy laughs again.

"How is it my fault?"

April points at Hardy with a knowing look.

"You're too damn hot for your own good Hardy—I tried but couldn't resist you. You used my weakness to your benefit knowing I'd give into your demands eventually. That day in the supermarket was the last straw. You wore those old Levi's on purpose didn't you? Your erection was all I could think of as we talked and then I couldn't help myself anymore—I knew you wanted to fuck me and I gave myself to you on your terms."

Hardy makes a lewd gesture with his finger.

"That's such bull. You wanted me as much as I wanted you that day and we did what came naturally despite me having a relationship with Natalie—the last few weeks have been quite the experience—no wonder precious Father William stumbled."

April seems upset and pushes Hardy away again.

"I thought I told you not to mention Father William's name again. He was not who I thought he was—he used me."

Hardy glances at the bedroom door.

"My bad—I'm sorry."

They look at each other.

"I promise I'll never bring up his name again."

April sighs loudly and lets her fingers slide gently along Hardy's cheek. He grins as her fingers pauses over his mouth.

"I think round two is necessary."

April glances at his erection and nods.

28

Wiley Wilkerson sighs loudly as he looks at the cell phone in his hand. He nods several times and seems a bit confused.

"I agree—it seems like an open and shut case."

He glances at the images on his cell phone briefly as a woman's picture appears. He shakes his head several times.

"She certainly has a lot of explaining to do."

He gestures with his hand and sighs.

"Drive safely."

He shuts off his cell phone.

"Never thought I'd hear from Edward Rolling again after I stole his girl in college and married her. Those were the days."

He begins laughing as he leans back in his chair.

29
Los Angeles

Edward steps into his car and shuts the door. He starts the engine seconds later. He seems in a crazed rush as he drives out of the parking lot and heads toward the San Diego Freeway.

TO BE CONTINUED

A Brief Look at the Final Episode

More secrets from the past reveal themselves as selected events prove that not everything is what it seems while a determined politician gets closer to finding out what took place several years before that resulted in the tragic death of his troubled sibling.

If Tomorrow Comes

1
Four Days Later

"I'm so sorry Enrique."

Laura Stryker wipes tears from her eyes as she faces Enrique Lopez. He seems confused as he looks at her while they sit inside a jail cell. He slowly runs his fingers through his hair.

"Why didn't you tell me?"

Laura sighs loudly.

"I tried but I just couldn't. I wanted to forget it ever happened. Steve Rolling was a drug dealer and thief when I met him. I was at such a low point in my life at that time I let myself be taken in by his charms—and then things went from bad to worse for me. He beat me all the time and threatened if I left him he'd kill me—made it clear he had killed several people before."

Enrique shakes his head.

"Why didn't you talk to his brother?"

Laura sighs again.

"I didn't know he had a brother."

She begins to cry again.

"He never talked about his family. He never told me anything about his past—except for having an aunt that was suffering from terminal cancer or something. She was practically comatose when I met her. The day he died we were at her house and he was going through her jewelry collection—looking for anything he could fence—and then things went horribly wrong and he ended up dead. It was a tragic accident—he attacked me when I tried to leave so I hit him over the head with a vase."

Enrique reaches out to put his arms around Laura.

"What happened after that?"

Laura slowly turns to face Enrique.

"I panicked when I realized he was dead and fled."

She shakes her head.

"I had been questioned by the cops before Steve died and I knew it was only a matter of time before the pieces were put together by someone so I decided to leave Los Angeles."

She touches Enrique's hand.

"I took the first taxi I could find and decided to head north and then I saw a sign for Ocean Landing and decided this might be the place where I could rebuild my life. I'd already lived here as a kid and knew the layout pretty well. Of course I had baggage from what had happened at the inn previously but I decided it was still better than venturing all the way to San Francisco."

Enrique notices Simon Andrews and Colin Baxter talking several feet away in the hallway with Edward Rolling and Wiley Wilkerson. He faces Laura again and slides his hand into hers.

"This will work out—you'll see."

He turns to look at the hallway once more.

2

"I see you're feeling better."

Ward Brady grins as he pulls Larisa Lopez toward him and kisses her. He makes a lewd gesture with his hand and grins.

"I'm back on the road to recovery no doubt."

Larisa kisses Ward again.

"I thought I'd lost you—I was so scared."

Ward grins slyly.

"Do you know what I'm thinking about right now?"

Larisa pretends to slap him.

"We're not having sex in a hospital room."

Ward rolls his eyes.

"I'm horny."

Larisa pushes him away.

"The doctor said you're not to have sex for the next week or two. Doctor Benning was very clear about that. Said you needed to regain your strength unimpeded. Case closed."

Ward seems disappointed.

"What does he know?"

Larisa wags her finger at him.

"He saved your life—gave you back to me."

Larisa kisses Ward on the cheek.

"Your mother said Claire was placed in a padded cell—said she tried to kill herself after she was arrested. Kept saying you fathered her unborn child—and that I caused you to cheat."

Ward makes a gesture with his hand.

"None of that happened—except in Claire's mind. Once I caught her cheating it was over between us. She was never pregnant except in her own fantasies. We split up long before I met you—you had nothing to do with her behavior. I filed for divorce right before we began dating. Claire's delusions made her lose her grip on reality—she projected her behavior onto me in order to be able to live with herself and what she did after she ended up alone. I loved her at one time but infidelity is something I can't deal with. I was always faithful—never strayed. She did."

Larisa tousles Ward's hair.

"Sensitive guy aren't you?"

Ward nods and gives Larisa a sly look.

"I still want to have sex."

Larisa pretends to slap Ward again. He grins and wags his finger at her. She reaches out to tousle his hair and laughs.

"Not one more word about having sex."

Larisa gives Ward a warning look and smiles.

"Not happening today—not happening for the next week either—doctor's orders—it's the way things are gonna be."

Ward seems disappointed and sighs loudly.

3

"I want her sent back to Los Angeles."

Edward looks at Wiley. He sighs.

"I want her to pay."

Wiley runs his fingers through his hair.

"Did you read the report?"

"I did—all lies."

Wiley guides Edward toward a nearby car in the parking lot. They stop. Wiley glances at the police station and shrugs.

"Laura Stryker passed a lie detector test."

"So what—those things aren't guaranteed. She killed him in cold blood. I want her to rot in prison for what she did."

Wiley grabs Edward by the shoulders.

"I wouldn't count on this thing going to trial. Your brother left plenty of witnesses to his behavior with Laura. They have all agreed that he was abusive. Steve's death was an accident."

He sighs loudly.

"A terrible accident—but nevertheless an accident of which no jury will be able to see otherwise—it's over."

Edward clenches his fists angrily.

"I want her behind bars."

Wiley looks at the police station again.

"They're going to release her tomorrow morning."

Edward seems about to explode.

4

Gary Barrington notices Susan Balfour exiting a pharmacy nearby and grins broadly. He walks over to her and smirks.

"Hello Susan—nice day isn't it?"

Susan looks at Gary coldly and quickly walks by him without saying a word. He laughs and continues walking.

"I guess she's still upset about Rodney."

He laughs again.

"Oh well—if that's the way she wants to play."

He turns to look at Susan once more.

5

"I got here as soon as I could."

Larisa looks in shock as Sandra King comes toward her from the hallway of the hospital. They embrace warmly.

"I'm glad Ward is OK."

Larisa hugs Sandra again.

"Where's Scott?"

Sandra seems upset.

"He's in Los Angeles for some story Roland sent him to cover. Something about a drug-addicted television host."

Larisa makes a gesture with her hand.

"Tell him I said hi."

Sandra nods.

"I will."

She turns to see Malcolm Brady walking into Ward's room. Sandra faces Larisa with a wicked glint in her eye.

"Ward's brother is really easy on the eyes."

Larisa nods in agreement.

"He's got a good heart too—he'll make some woman a wonderful husband one day—been here since the beginning."

Sandra looks at her cell phone nervously.

"When you called you said Ward was not out of the woods yet. Is everything OK? Do you need a specialist or something? I could have someone come to Ocean Landing if necessary."

Larisa shakes her head and smiles.

"Ward has made a complete turnaround since I called you initially. He's already in the *mood* if you know what I mean."

Sandra grins broadly and nods.

"I'm glad he's OK—he'll be back to his old self in no time and perhaps the two of you can resume talk about starting a family. I know from what you said he wants to be a father."

Larisa smiles broadly.

6

Jesse Malinger backs away as Lance Marler circles him in a parking lot several yards away from a rocky cove as he proudly brandishes a gun and points it at Jesse. Lance grins broadly as he takes a step closer. He glances at the gun and laughs.

"Gunshot wounds can be so messy."

He grins slyly.

"Closed casket funeral without a doubt."

He takes another step.

"You seriously fucked with the wrong guy this time—and that foolish mistake will cost you dearly. One you're out of the way I'll have Sabrina where I want her. She'll beg me for mercy once I show her exactly what kind of guy I am. You caused me enough problems—ever since you came to town you've done things you shouldn't—but stealing my girl was the last straw."

He looks at the gun again.

"There's nowhere to run—time's up."

Lance laughs.

"I'm going to enjoy blowing you away."

He laughs again.

"No one can save your miserable life now loser—I win and you lose—say your prayers—I'm gonna love snuffing you out."

He kisses the gun several times.

"I should've killed you months ago."

He grins broadly.

"Say goodnight hotshot."

Jesse notices a steel pole lying against some shrubbery not far away and as Lance takes another step he grabs the pole and swings it at Lance. Caught off guard Lance drops the gun.

"Say your prayers fucker."

They scramble for the gun and as Lance tries to rip it from Jesse's hand it goes off. They look at each other in shock.

"Goddamn frigging bastard."

He sighs loudly.

"I hate you."

Lance looks at the gaping wound in his chest and falls backwards. Jesse reacts realizing he's covered in blood.

"Lance?"

There is no answer. Jesse panics and pulls out his cell phone. He begins dialing as he looks at Lance again. His skin changes color as Jesse begins yelling for help. From out of nowhere Daniel Williams jumps over a railing bordering the parking lot and runs toward Jesse. He looks at Lance and then at Jesse. The gun is lying on the ground a few feet away. Seconds later sirens are heard as David Kipling pulls up in a patrol car.

7

Lana Collins stops at the doorway leading to Ward's room and sighs. He notices and motions her over to his bed.

"You're my hero."

Lana seems confused.

"Me? What did I do?"

Ward looks at Larisa and then at Lana.

"I heard how you grabbed the gun from Claire."

Lana shrugs and smiles weakly.

"I don't remember doing that to tell the truth—everything is a blur—it all happened so fast. I just did it without thinking."

Ward sits up in bed and grins.

"Modest too—I like that in a hero."

He gestures with his hand.

"I'll never forget what you did."

Lana shakes her head just as Malcolm enters.

"Have you asked her?"

Malcolm shoots Ward a cautious look and seems upset as he comes into the room. He gives Ward a knowing look.

"You stole my thunder big brother."
Lana turns to look at Malcolm and then at Larisa.
"What's going on?"
Malcolm walks over to Ward's bed.
"My big mouth brother jumped the gun as usual."
Lana glances back and forth between Larisa and Ward as Malcolm leads Lana outside the room and into the hallway.
"I was going to ask you to have dinner with me."
Lana reacts.
"You were going to ask me out?"
Malcolm nods.
"That was the plan."
Lana glances at Larisa and Ward. Larisa grins broadly.
"Well? What about it?"
Lana turns to look at Malcolm again.
"Sure. Of course I will."
Malcolm grins broadly.
"Six o'clock OK?"
Lana nods.

8

Wiley watches Edward's reaction. He seems in shock as he clenches his fist several times. Wiley turns to look back at the police station and then back at Edward. Wiley sighs loudly.

"Steve's death was an accident."

Edward grits his teeth.

"I don't believe a word that woman says. She killed him and made up this lurid tale about my brother. He was no saint by any means but he would never steal from a dying woman—I just won't accept he was that cold. She's no good—she used him like she's using that guy with her right now inside the station. He's in for a rude awakening the minute he crosses her. That woman is pure evil—my brother never had a chance. She killed him."

Wiley shakes his head several times and leans against Edward's car. He watches as Edward clenches his fist again.

"This isn't right. Someone has to be held accountable for what happened to Steve. There has to be something I can do."

Wiley slowly runs his fingers through his hair.

"Keep in touch OK?"

Edward nods and gets into the car.

9
Salt Lake City

"Uh-huh—that's right. Dennis Bosley was not his real name. Dennis was a childhood friend that was killed in a boating accident when he was nine. My brother must have assumed Dennis Bosley's identity after his initial arrest for attempted murder during his first year of college. He disappeared right after and I thought he had long since passed. But then I saw your story about a serial killer named Dennis Bosley two days ago."

Matthew Leigh sighs loudly as he watches the reaction of the woman looking back at him on the screen. Jill Edmondson remains silent for a few seconds. Finally she snaps out of the shock she seems to be adjusting to and faces Matthew again.

"How are your parents handling the news?"

Matthew gestures with his hand.

"Truthfully it comes as no surprise that he led this sort of life. They tried to get him committed after his arrest but they were hamstrung by how the law works in this country."

He sighs loudly and takes a deep breath.

"By the time they were able to make headway my brother had vanished. From that moment Gregory Leigh became Dennis and started killing people up and down the coast of Oregon and California. I'm sure there are more victims than the ones already reported. My brother was quite sadistic—liked inflicting pain."

Jill reacts and looks at the photographs of Gregory on the screen as Matthew watches her reaction. She leans back in her chair and spends a few seconds seemingly lost in thought.

"Do you think there are possible survivors? Someone who might have somehow escaped—witnesses to his behavior?"

Matthew shakes his head and seems unsure as he loads a few more photographs onto the computer. He sighs loudly.

"Possibly—but knowing my brother I doubt he would leave someone behind who could identify him. He didn't like taking chances—always preferred a sure thing. Killing anyone who could expose him later was almost guaranteed. My brother was quite twisted in case that part of his profile wasn't reflected in the police reports surrounding his demise earlier this year."

Jill nods and folds her hands in front of her.

"Is it possible you could come to Ocean Landing? Or I could come to Salt Lake. I'd like to interview you. Really delve into this story—help people make sense of what happened."

Matthew nods. He glances back toward the door to his office and stifles a laugh. He holds up a few picture frames.

"Salt Lake would be better without a doubt. As you long as you can stomach my twins. But be warned—they are quite the menace. They just began to walk and are into everything."

Jill begins laughing and nods.

"I'm good with toddlers—don't worry."

Matthew grins broadly.

10

"I thought I made myself clear I wasn't going to tolerate you scoping out the girls in this town—it's time I taught you a lesson—one that you won't soon forget. Goddamn runt."

Emerson Wilkerson looks up to see Mark Gilpin standing inches away with a nasty scowl on his face. Emerson glances at the other patrons in the diner. He stands up and faces Mark and Veronica Cabot. He watches as Mark and Veronica exchange glances. Emerson looks around at the other patrons again.

"I'll look at whomever I want—and if you and that punk you call your boyfriend have anything to say about it—fuck you and him too—yeah—I'll do as I please—you don't scare me."

Emerson laughs and points at Mark.

"Uh-huh—I've heard the chatter about you."

He turns to face Veronica and smirks.

"Talk about town is that your guy here is gay—likes boys not girls. Ugh—can't you see him for what he is—a pansy."

Veronica reacts at the comment. Mark grabs Emerson and seems about to hit him. Emerson begins laughing gleefully.

"Are you gonna kiss me or kick my ass?"

Mark notices a few people have gathered and seem to be looking at him oddly. He suddenly lets go of Emerson.

"I'm not gay—ask anyone."

Emerson turns to Victoria and grins.

"Is he or isn't he?"

She seems unable to answer.

11

Los Angeles

A covered body is wheeled toward a waiting coroner's van while Patrick Irvington seems to stifle a smile as he closes the front door of a small bungalow. He turns to face the officer standing a few feet away. He wipes sweat from his brow.

"Terribly tragic how some people choose to end their lives—even if they're one of ours. Masters had everything to live for but still he decided to put an end to everything with a single bullet. His immediate family in Burbank will be heartbroken."

The officer nods in agreement as Patrick turns away and grins broadly. He walks toward a patrol car a few feet away.

"I guess Masters wished now that he hadn't threatened me the way he did—oh well—things happen. People die."

He begins to laugh.

"Got to call Cujo and thank him for his superb work making Leonard's death look like a tragic case of suicide."

He reaches for his cell phone and smiles. Seconds later he sees Cujo Momoa staring back at him as he sits by a pool.

"I thought I'd call and say thanks for what you did on such short notice. Leonard Masters was a loose end that had to be dealt with before he ruffled the wrong feathers in this city."

Cujo takes a sip from a can of beer in his hand and grins as he stands and looks out at the other end of the pool where two scantily glad women are lounging. He makes a lewd gesture with his finger as he faces Patrick again. He begins laughing.

"We're gonna party for the next several hours I guarantee you—love how things have gone. Masters is no longer an issue to be worried about. Those files will never see the light of day."

Patrick gestures with his hand.

"I assume you destroyed all the files?"

Cujo nods and grins broadly.

14

Natalie MacDonald sighs loudly as she knocks on the front door of Hardy's apartment. From inside she hears voices and calls out. But there is no reply. She slowly reaches out and grabs the doorknob. She pushes the door forward. As she enters laughter can be heard coming from the hallway. She closes the door behind her and stops cold as the sounds become louder. Natalie storms toward the hallway and in a rage flings open the bedroom door. She sees Hardy Wheeler lying on top of April Estes ramming her unaware Natalie is standing a few feet away. Hardy turns to face her as April grins and blows Natalie a kiss.

"I was gonna tell you."

Natalie turns and bolts from the room as Hardy turns to look at April again. He laughs as he resumes kissing her.

"Can you believe her—how rude?"

April giggles and gestures with her hand.

12

"You really did a job on Mark earlier. He's a sorry mess."

Emerson turns to look at Veronica and grins slyly. She nervously sits down next to Emerson. He turns to face her.

"He had it coming. That freak is pathetic—he and Marler are cut from the same cloth. They think they own the world."

"Is Mark Gilpin really gay? I had no idea he liked guys."

Emerson makes a lewd gesture with his finger and sighs.

"I made the whole thing up—played him."

Veronica seems impressed and smiles broadly.

"He and I aren't that close anyway."

Emerson glances at the front door of the diner seemingly bored with Veronica's sudden change of attitude. He sighs.

"I could use a girl like you in my life."

Veronica is about to reach out to touch Emerson's hand when Andy Archer comes toward her. He seems in shock.

13

Gary looks at Helene Jeffreys and grins broadly. She slowly begins to unbutton his Levi's as his erection seems ready to break free at any moment. He sighs loudly as she kisses the buttons several times and looks up at him. Gary laughs loudly with glee as her fingers linger over each button. As his penis comes into view amid a thick puff of pubic hair he watches her reaction and smirks. He sighs as her tongue seductively slides across the massive expanse of his penis. He moans loudly as she begins giving him a sensuous blowjob less than a minute later.

One Day Later

15

"I can't believe it's finally over."

Laura takes Enrique's hand and they begin walking down the steps of the police station as several reporters suddenly descend on them. Laura stops and faces the cameras.

About the Series Creator

Gary Brin was born in 1965 and has lived in the United States Virgin Islands, Hawaii and California. He has edited numerous original literary works over the years—both new and revised. In 2019 he established Standish Press to bring forth interesting fictional and historical material usually ignored by mainstream publishers because of specific views or content. In addition to publishing books, he also created the Nancy Hanks Lincoln Public Library (named after the mother of Abraham Lincoln) in 2014 to make available hard-to-find books to a worldwide audience.

Production Notes

Written by Wesley Adams and Daphne McGee
Manuscript edited by Gary Brin
Cover photograph from Wikimedia Commons
Front cover design and interior book layout by Gary Brin
Cover layout by Victoria Valentine
Additional help provided by Carlton J. Young
Series created by Gary Brin

Character List

Marlene Alderson
Alison Allington
Ben Allington
Jacob Allington
Simon Andrews
Andy Archer
Nancy Baker
Susan Balfour
Gary Barrington
Colin Baxter
Carter Benning
Charles Benning
Gina Bertinelli
Andrew Brady
Claire Brady
Malcolm Brady
Ward Brady
Veronica Cabot
Julie Cartwright
Lana Collins
Cheryl Cooke
Laird Cooke
Mason Crumble
Chase Doubleday
Jill Edmondson
April Estes
Karen Ewing
Kyle Fairgate
Kyle Garland
Racine Gilbert
Mark Gilpin
Bernard Grable

Patrick Irvington
Helene Jeffreys
Sandra King
David Kipling
Kevin Kulkovich
Matthew Leigh
Larisa Lopez
Marta Lopez
Sergei Lycov
Natalie MacDonald
Jesse Malinger
Lance Marler
Rebecca Martin
Leonard Masters
Sherilyn Matthews
Sabrina McCord
Cujo Momoa
Maureen O'Bannon
Diana Ordway
Lloyd Ordway
Maxwell Pendergraft
Travis Penwick
Bastian Rego
Cynthia Rodgers
Edward Rolling
Rodney Royer
Wesley Royer
David Sherwood
Jennifer Slater
Cyril Spalding
Carly Spellman
Laura Stryker
Astrid Thomas
Dexter Thomas
Jeffrey Webber
Hardy Wheeler
Robert Widdemer

Emerson Wilkerson
Wiley Wilkerson
Yvette Wilkerson
Daniel Williams
Greg Williams
Erica Wynne
Dorothea Wong
Jared Wycroft
Paul Yarmouth
Todd Zimmer

**Real People, Real
Animals, and Historical
Events Mentioned**

John Alden
Black Dahlia
Bob the Cat
James Bowen
William Bradford
William Brewster
Julia Child
Jamie Lee Curtis
Bobby Fuller
Irene Garza
Tom Hiddleston
Tom Holland
Robert Kennedy
Jayne Mansfield
Nicholas Markowitz
Marilyn Monroe
Martha Moxley
Robert Piest
Pilgrims
Glen Albert Pritchett
Gordon Ramsay
George Reeves

Paul Revere
Hal Roach
Salem Witch Trials
Tom Selleck
Marc Singer
Myles Standish
John Steinbeck
William Desmond Taylor
Thelma Todd
Luke Treadaway
Robert Wagner
War of Independence
Jacob Wetterling
Natalie Wood

Next in the Series
Book 8
Marble Hills

OCEAN LANDING

Published by
Standish Press